I0603821

Shoot to Kill

A Hollywood Murder, Book 3

Cynthia Hickey

DEDICATION

To God for the endless story ideas, to my husband for his never-ending support, and to all the cozy mystery lovers waiting for the next story.

To all my readers. I wouldn't be doing the job I love without you.

Chapter One

I was dead. Deceased. About to be buried. I, Kelly Canyon, wannabe crime reporter, current actor and photographer, stared at the brand-spanking new, hot-red Jimmy Choos hanging from my dog's mouth. Grandma, or Ruthie, as she preferred to be called, was going to kill me and Shutterbug. "Drop it, girl." What was with my normally well-trained dog and shoes?

Ruthie marched into the room, set her Yorkie, Sassy, on the sofa and pointed at Shutterbug. "Drop them this instant."

The shoes fell to the floor with a thud. Shutterbug's ears perked-up and she tilted her head to the side, looking very pleased with herself.

"I'm sorry, Ruthie." I grinned sheepishly. "We were just about to head out the door to scope out the venue for the award's ceremony when she trotted out of your room with these."

"The very shoes I plan on wearing to receive my award." Ruthie snatched the shoes from the floor and flipped them over in her hands. "Nothing but drool." She wagged a finger at Shutterbug. "You are one lucky dog." With her nose in the air, Ruthie whirled and marched to her room.

"At least we're still breathing." I snapped my fingers for my furry best friend to follow me outside. Since it was just the two of us, I buckled her into the passenger seat of my 1965 candy apple red Corvette. Soon, we were zooming toward Hollywood Boulevard.

Ruthie was going to receive a lifetime achievement award. With our most recent season of our mother/daughter cop drama, her fame had grown. Well, mine too, but I much preferred the attention I received from writing a book based on each of the last two murders I'd help solve. Book number one stayed on the best-seller list and I had high hopes for book two. Soon, I wouldn't have to act and could devote all my time to photography and writing.

Yes, I'd given up on becoming a crime reporter. I got paid more from being an author and still took photographs for fun and a little pocket money, as Ruthie called it.

I'd volunteered to take photos at the award ceremony where Ruthie would receive the award. Brock was emceeing the event and would be more handsome than was legal. I still couldn't believe he called me his girlfriend.

I parked behind the theater and let Shutterbug out of the car. She dashed ahead of me, stopping at the door with an excited yip. I smiled, spotting Brock's car. He'd arrived first and probably had Brutus with him. Good. The dogs could play while we worked.

Brutus, an English Mastiff around six months old would catch up in size to Shutterbug very soon. The gangly pup barreled toward us. The only thing that kept me from being bowled over was Shutterbug leaping between us to play.

"Good morning." Brock strolled my way, a smile highlighting his handsome features.

"Good morning." I lifted my face for his kiss. "Been scoping out the best places for your promo pics?"

He obliged with the kiss. "I think I've found a few places that will work. Let's see what your expert eyes say." He slid his arm around my waist.

A few minutes later, we entered a dressing room. "I thought maybe one of me in front of the mirror for makeup. Then another of me in my tux and maybe a few candid pictures of me on stage just hanging around in my jeans and tee shirt."

I nodded. The candid ones would be the best. Brock looked very good in jeans and a tee shirt. "Maybe a couple of you and Brutus?"

"If we can get him to sit still long enough. He's got enough energy for three dogs."

"Shutterbug got Ruthie's shoes again." I sagged onto a chaise lounge. "I might have to get my own place."

He sat next to me. "Not in a million years. Ruthie would never kick you or Shutterbug out. Despite her grumbles, she loves your dog almost as much as that yappy thing she takes everywhere with her."

A few months back, I'd bought Ruthie the Yorkie pup to ease her loneliness when I wasn't around. Brock had found Brutus around the same time, and life became pretty chaotic with three dogs under one year in age. I wouldn't trade a minute of it. Then, to spite the local law enforcement who often accused me of interfering, all three of us had our pups certified as service dogs so they could go with us everywhere. Shutterbug had proven her worth already by taking down a criminal.

"Let's get started," I said, "I need to read over my script for next season. We start filming on Monday." Today was Friday and the ceremony tonight, but weekends often got away from me. Not entirely true. The beach called to me way too often on the weekends for me to get any reading done.

Brock led the way to the stage and whistled for Brutus. The pup lumbered down the aisle and bounded onto the stage.

I took a few shots of Brock and the pup wrestling, then some posed ones of them on the stage steps, before taking a few of Brock alone. Not an easy thing to do with a large puppy that wanted to photobomb the shoot.

The ones of Brock having his makeup done and wearing his tux would have to wait until after the ceremony that night. He wore makeup now, but fans liked to see the process of getting Hollywood glam, so we'd pretend. I packed up my camera and studied the room. Plush red chairs faced the stage. A matching carpet runner ran down the aisle, promising that everyone who entered would receive the royal treatment. The venue wasn't as large as the one that housed the Oscars, but still impressive with two thousand seats and a balcony that held a thousand more.

"Is Leo's catering?" I glanced at Brock.

"Yep. Let's hope the night doesn't end with a crab leg in someone's neck." He shuddered.

"Don't remind me." I'd thought the death of Lauren Matthews to have been my first experience with murder, but I couldn't have been more wrong. It was my second. My father's death was the first, as it turned out. Then the maintenance man, Bob, was the third. A movie studio or random traffic stop couldn't prevent evil doings.

Later that evening, I hung back as Brock escorted Ruthie up the red carpet. I wasn't his date this time. Just like a year ago, I was a member of those photographers, hungrily snapping pix of the arriving celebrities. The only change…I could focus this time on Brock and Ruthie and didn't have to rely on selling the photos to pay my bills. Also, like a year ago, I had a special pass to get into the theater and go anywhere I pleased.

Which I did. I slipped away from the crowd the moment Brock and Ruthie stepped into the theater and made my way around to the back door. After flashing my ID badge to the muscled guard, I entered the building and headed for Brock's room. He would be the only star receiving makeup.

Everyone else would take their seats immediately.

"Hey, Lisa." I greeted the artist who did Ruthie's and my makeup for our show. "I'm glad they let you do Brock."

"Me, too." She held out a trembling hand. "I've never worked on someone so gorgeous before. What if I mess up?"

"Don't think of him as Mr. Handsome." I plopped on the lounge. "Think of him as a pesky neighbor kid with an annoying dog."

"I heard that." Brock entered and came straight to me for a kiss before flashing Lisa a grin. "I don't bite."

Instead of calming her, his smile made her more nervous. "I know," she said softly. "Good grief. I can hack into computers, erase dark shadows under a person's eyes, so I think I can do a simple makeup job."

"Good. If my agent hadn't insisted I look my best under the harsh lights, I'd skip this part." He sat in the chair and raised his chin so she could put an apron around his neck.

I snapped a few photos, then sat back and enjoyed feasting my eyes on a man as gorgeous inside as out. No wonder fans called him Hollywood's Golden Boy. Not because of his looks, not because of his almost black hair and sky-blue eyes, but because of his kindness.

He caught me feasting and gave me that tender smile he reserved for me. The one that sent my heart into flips.

"Ready?" I stood and handed him the tuxedo hanging on a rod. "I'll wait outside and walk with you to the stage."

"Great." He glanced in the mirror. "You did a super job, Lisa. The lights won't wash me out."

Her eyes widened. "Does that mean I went too dark?"

He chuckled. "You did just right."

She exhaled heavily. "Great. It'll look good on my resume to add your name." She flashed a grin, then hurried from the room.

"You look like you have a tan," I whispered on my way out the door.

His laugh followed. True to form, Brock hadn't wanted to hurt her feelings. While he possessed enough ego to fit into Hollywood, he was also humble enough not to hurt someone's feelings. God broke the mold when he made Brock Hanson.

I reached over and toggled the light switch on the hall to get some good lighting when Brock exited his room. The hall remained dim, lit by a single light in the direction of the stage.

This wouldn't work at all. I flagged down a man in dark blue coveralls. "This light isn't working."

"So?" He pulled the brim of his cap down lower over his eyes.

"It's too dark. I can't see you, and you're only an arm's length away. How am I supposed to take pictures?"

"Fine. Follow me." He led me in the opposite direction to a dead end. We turned and headed down another hall.

"Do you know where we're going?"

"No, I'm new. I'm looking for the fuse box and got turned around. There it is." He opened a green metal box on the wall and flipped a couple of switches.

The hall behind us blazed to life. "That's bright enough to land a plane. Will that work?"

"Yes."

He rushed away, leaving me alone. The dude might be maintenance, at least that's what he looked like, but the man was plain rude.

I slammed the door to the fuse box and turned to leave. Brock would be ready to go, and we were cutting it close to showtime.

Something caught my attention from the corner of my eye. I turned and glanced behind a large cement post used to support the floor above. A man sat against the concrete block wall. A knife protruded from his white tee shirt-covered chest, and blood ran into the waistband of his green plaid boxer shorts.

Chapter Two

Past experience told me to call Detective Lawrence before anything else. "I, uh, found a dead body." I kneeled down to check for a pulse in his neck just to make sure. "He's still warm."

Lawrence's sigh vibrated through the airwaves. "Of course, you did. I'll be there in two minutes. I'm coming up the walk now."

"You are?"

"I have an invitation from Ruthie."

I guess my grandmother accepted the fact that my father and Lori Lawrence had a relationship before his death. The detective was now as determined as I was to find out who killed him.

A few minutes later, Lori strolled toward me looking stunning in a deep burgundy evening gown. She swished the hem to the side and bent over the body. "Where are his clothes?"

"I think the man who led me back here stole them."

She straightened. "You'll need to explain a little more than that." She spun toward Brock as he hurried toward us.

"What happened?" He glanced down. "Oh, no."

"Yes, it appears Kelly has stumbled upon another murder. Please proceed with the ceremony as planned, Brock. We don't need a panicked crowd or a bunch of looky-loos." She'd started calling me by my first name after letting me know how much she loved my father.

Brock nodded, cast one more glance my way, then headed to the stage, acting as if nothing was happening in the halls of the building.

The moment he left, words spewed out of my mouth. "The lights were out at this end of the hall making it too dark for me to take good shots of Brock leaving his dressing room. I found a man in a maintenance uniform to turn on the lights…"

"You followed a stranger into a dark hallway?"

"In my defense, I thought he worked here." I crossed my arms.

Lori lifted her dress, revealing a gun and a cell phone strapped to her thigh. She placed a call to her new partner, Detective Warren, before speaking again. "The perp wouldn't steal a uniform and kill the man who wore it unless he had something else planned. If he wanted this man dead, and nothing more, he would have simply killed him."

Nothing about murder was simple, but I saw her point. "We need to find that man." My heart dropped to my toes. Who was the target?

"Go take pictures of the crowd. Quickly. I need to know which celebrity he's after."

I nodded and raced for the stage. Once there, I hooked my telephoto lens onto my camera and snapped photos of every corner of the room.

Brock cut a quick glance my way but never faltered in listing the nominees for best supporting actor. His smile dazzled. His jokes made the audience laugh. He kept them enthralled while I tried to find the killer's next victim before they became one.

The whole time I took photos I expected a shot to ring out or a scream to echo. When I'd taken all the pictures I could, I hurried back to Lori.

By this time her partner had arrived. "Canyon's at it again."

I rolled my eyes. "You make it sound like I'm the killer."

He shrugged.

"Give me the camera." Lori snatched it from me and scrolled through the photos.

"Be careful. That's expensive." I peered over her shoulder. "I don't see anyone other than those involved in the movie industry. Which one could be the target?"

"I don't know." She scrolled through them again with more urgency. "Warren, stand with Kelly on the stage. I'll take my place at the back of the auditorium. Keep your eyes peeled. Kelly, keep scanning the crowd with your telephoto. We have to find this guy. He won't be out in the open wearing a coverall. He'll find a place to hide."

Detective Warren wasn't someone I'd pick to

stakeout with, seeming to have no sense of humor and a perpetual scowl on his face, but since I wasn't a police officer, I couldn't make an arrest if we did find the killer. I resolved to pretend he wasn't breathing over my shoulder and headed for the stage as two uniformed cops took up residence over the body.

Lori's heels tapped out a fast rhythm as she headed for the auditorium. When I resumed my spot behind the curtains, I caught sight of her standing in the back of the room, her dark gown almost blending in with the wall. She had the perfect vantage spot and wasn't immediately noticed.

Rather than focus my lens on the audience, this time I scanned the outside perimeter. My heart lodged in my throat as Brock announced my grandmother's name.

Movement on the balcony caught my attention and I focused my camera in that direction. "Warren. There."

He jumped off the stage, shouting into his radio.

Lori headed for the stairs.

Brock glanced at me, then to the balcony as Ruthie stepped up to the microphone.

"Ruthie!" I darted toward her as the man above us raised a gun.

Brock didn't hesitate. He tackled my grandmother to the ground, shielding her with his body, using the podium as cover.

The gun switched its aim to me.

I dove to the floor as the shot rang out, not taking my eyes off the man trying to kill me.

The room erupted into pandemonium and

screams as those in attendance converged on the exits. The shooter disappeared into an alcove.

"Kelly?" Brock's gaze bore into mine.

"I'm okay." Actually, I'd fallen on my camera and had the breath knocked from me. I'd be sporting a bad bruise, but I was alive. So, yeah, I was okay.

Brock helped Ruthie to her feet, and the three of us took shelter behind the stage backdrop. "Why would someone want to kill the two of you?"

"Not me. Ruthie. I was an afterthought. Otherwise, he would have killed me when he had me alone." Dread trickled down my spine.

Ruthie clutched her throat. "Why would anyone want to kill me?"

"That's what we need to find out."

Footsteps sounded behind us and Brock positioned himself between Ruthie and me and possible danger.

"Relax." Lori, with Warren right behind her, stepped from behind the curtain. "The shooter got away. We need to get you two out of here."

Lori and Warren formed a barrier in front of us with Brock behind and led us through a side exit of the building and into the back of Warren's car. "We'll collect your vehicles at daylight." Lori shut us in, then stepped back as Warren slid into the driver's seat.

Seconds later we sped from the parking lot toward home. No one said a word. My mind whirled, searching for a reason someone would want my grandmother dead, and I couldn't come up with a single one.

At home, Warren rushed us inside and locked the door before racing around the main room to close all the blinds. When he finished, he took up a position near the front door and stared at the back wall of windows, wincing with each of Shutterbug's growls. She never had grown to like the man. "You need curtains on those."

"I like being able to see out," Ruthie said.

"No offense, ma'am, but someone just tried to kill you. This wall of windows gives them the perfect opportunity."

She shrugged and headed for her room. "I'm changing out of this dress."

My heart ached for her. Not only had someone tried to shoot her, but she hadn't received the award that meant so much to her. She'd still get it, but not with her peers looking on. From exotic dancer to actress to mother taking time off to raise her son and granddaughter, then back to actress, Ruthie hadn't received a lot of accolades in her life. She needed this.

A knock sounded at the door. Warren peered through the peephole, then opened the door to let Lori, now dressed in navy slacks and a white blouse, inside.

She glanced around the room. "Where's Ruthie?"

"In her room changing," I said.

"I don't want her alone." She hurried down the hall.

I met Brock's worried gaze. "Want to help me make coffee?"

He nodded and followed me to the kitchen.

"Does Ruthie seem a little calm to you?"

"Come to think of it, yes. She was more worried a few months ago at being blackmailed." I lowered my voice. "She doesn't seem surprised, does she?"

"Not as much as I'd expect her to be." He pressed the button to turn on the coffeepot. "Why is that?"

"I'm not sure, but she doesn't talk about her past much. Could it be something in relation to that?"

"Or my father's death," which was easier to believe.

Ruthie entered the kitchen, Sassy tucked under one arm, and dropped a bright-colored file with fluorescent flowers across the front. "A week before his death, your father gave me these papers and told me to hide them away."

"That folder did not belong to Dad." I eyed the highlighted-yellow folder.

"No, but I thought if the papers were that important, no one would think to look in something so girly."

I opened the folder. Inside were pages and pages of letters and numbers. "Code? Please tell me you made copies."

"What do you think I've been doing? It doesn't take this long to change clothes."

"Where's Lori?" I peeked down the hall.

"Waiting for me to come out of the restroom." Ruthie grinned. "I don't think she knows I have two doors to that room."

"You'd better hurry back before she gets suspicious," Brock said. "We'll give this to her—"

"Give me what?" Lori entered the kitchen and

glared at Ruthie. "You could have told me you snuck out the back door."

"Sorry. I remembered this file and was in a hurry to give it to Kelly."

"It's in some kind of code." I handed Lori the folder. "Ruthie thinks the shooter might be targeting her because of this. Dad gave it to her right before he was killed."

Lori paled. "I know you have a copy. Keep it hidden. I'll take this one to the station with me to decipher it."

"What about Ruthie's protection?" Or mine, come to think about it.

"We'll have a uniformed guard out front at all times. He'll patrol the perimeter of the house at random times. Keep your alarm on and your dogs close." She tucked the folder under her arm and strode to the living room.

"What's that?" Warren glanced at the folder.

"A lead, I hope." She glanced back at us. "Keep your wits about you." With those words, she yanked open the door and left with Warren at her heels.

I studied the solemn faces of Brock and Ruthie. "We need to crack this code. Ruthie. Dad must have had the key somewhere."

"Key?"

"What the letters and numbers stand for. We need to find it. Where might he have hidden something like that?"

"In the old house."

"The one someone lives in now?"

She nodded. "How are we going to search there?"

"We make the owners an offer they can't refuse," Brock said.

Chapter Three

It took a week and half a million dollars to convince the owners of Ruthie's old house to sell. Still, my grandmother considered it money well spent if it helped solve Dad's murder.

"We'll keep it as rental property," she said. "Homes this close to the beach are in high demand."

Some might not consider five miles far, I guess. "How long did you give them to move out?"

"They said they could be out by the end of this week." She sighed and plopped onto the sofa, drawing Sassy onto her lap. "I've decided not to attend any more award ceremonies. Someone always gets killed."

I clicked a leash on Shutterbug's collar. "Not because you attend, Ruthie. Pure coincidence."

"Maybe not. Still doing the running thing, huh?"

"Yes. I'm trying to be consistent, and it gets Shutterbug the exercise she needs. I'll be back in a while. Stay inside, please."

She narrowed her eyes. "The man took a shot at you, Kelly."

"But it wasn't me he was after."

"You don't know that."

I planted a kiss on her cheek. "See you later." Before she could protest further, I dashed outside.

Running in our upscale, gated community didn't pose much danger. I waved at the cop in the navy sedan and kept on going, my feet pounding the pavement.

I'd run a lot as a teenager in high school and felt a great deal of pleasure at resuming the sport. Not only did it keep me fit, but it helped me think, and I had a lot of thinking to do.

We were between shooting seasons of our television show, and I had another week before needing to be back on set. There was no better way for me to spend that free week than finding out who wanted to kill Ruthie and what the papers she gave Lori were all about.

It sure turned out to be an expensive quest with Ruthie purchasing her old house. She could afford it, but I hoped it would be worth the money she spent.

Did the coded papers have anything to do with the police files dumped in an empty lot a few months ago? The files had led me to discover that Lori had a loving relationship with my father and also led me to suspect someone on the police force was dirty. Bribes? Protection money?

My thinking raised more questions than answers. I had no idea where to start solving the mystery except for searching the old house and talking again to my father's old cop friends. One in particular.

Morgan had been a big help in keeping us safe before, and it wasn't too hard to see he had strong feelings for Ruthie. Maybe he would know something about the coded pages.

I turned around at the corner and headed home to shower and change. If Morgan knew anything, he would help.

An hour later, I knocked on his door. "I need to hire you to protect Ruthie," I said the moment he answered.

"What happened?" He stepped back, allowing me to enter.

"Someone tried to kill her at the award ceremony last week. Brock managed to keep her safe, then the shooter's attention shifted to me." I explained about the coded pages and pulled them from my camera bag. "Do these mean anything to you?"

He scratched a couple days' growth of beard. "Maybe. I can't decipher them, but we both know your father was on to something."

My shoulders slumped. "I hoped you might be able to break the code."

"Well, I might. If I'm going to be staying at your place for a while, then I'll have time to work on it." He handed them back to me.

"You'll come?"

He glanced at me as if I'd said the dumbest thing, which I guess I had. "Stupid question. Hold on while I grab a few things. I'll follow you back since I doubt you brought a vehicle that will hold me, you, and the dog."

I grinned. "Nope, I drove the Camaro, not the Corvette. I'll even let you drive back."

"Sweet." He hurried out of sight, returning a few minutes later with a beat-up duffel bag. From the clunk it made when he set it on the coffee table, the bag held more than clothes.

Good. I tossed him the car keys and waited while he fetched another bag. All right, the man was prepared for anything.

"Let's go." He led the way outside, then swiveled and locked the door behind us. "Does Ruthie know I'm coming?"

I shook my head. "I actually expected to see more of you."

"I'm terrified of telling her how I feel. Besides, she needed time after finding out her last love was nothing more than a crook."

"Why? It's just Ruthie."

"Exactly."

I rolled my eyes. Morgan had been a regular when she danced for money, and despite her earlier risqué career, he had fallen deeply in love with her, although he'd kept his feelings to himself all these years.

"I think it's time you said something, you big baby."

"That I am." He tossed the bags into the backseat with Shutterbug, then climbed into the driver's seat, moving the seat back to accommodate his long legs. "Where's your fella?"

"Filming." With Brock being in high demand, I

didn't get to see much of him while I was on hiatus from the set. "He'll be over later."

My thoughts shifted back to the pages. "I think Dad was on to someone being paid protection money, and the pages are a list of those being protected."

"That's a good hunch."

I cut him a sideways glance. "What else could it be?"

"A report of dirty cops' doings."

I shrugged. "Either way, we're going to be searching Ruthie's old house next week to try and find the code key."

"You might want to put a bug in my sister's ear about finding out what happened to your father's old work desk."

"Lori would know. Good idea." I sent her a quick text and got an immediate response.

"It's in storage somewhere. Great idea. I'll look for it."

I typed, "I've hired Morgan as a bodyguard."

"Good."

I slipped my phone back in my bag. "She's going to look for his desk." We'd solve this case too, just like the last two murders.

The identity of the victim hadn't revealed any clues whatsoever. The poor man seemed to have been in the wrong place at the wrong time and convenient for the shooter. Luckily, he'd been unmarried with no children. Still, his death deserved justice.

Ruthie was lying out by the pool when we arrived. Morgan set his bags down, took a deep breath and sat in the lounge chair beside her. She removed dark sunglasses and smiled.

I couldn't hear their conversation from my position, but their body language told me Morgan had summoned the courage to tell Ruthie how he felt. I smiled and headed to the kitchen to fix the three of us some lunch.

By the time I cut up melon and made grilled ham and cheese with spinach, Morgan and Ruthie joined me inside. He tossed me a wink and held out a kitchen chair for Ruthie.

I mouthed, "I told you so" before carrying the tray with our lunches to the table.

"I've been thinking," Ruthie said.

"Uh-oh."

"Hush." She wadded up a napkin and tossed it at me. "I think I might know where to look in the old house."

"Really?" My eyebrows rose.

"That old shed at the far end of the yard."

I shuddered. "It's dark and full of bugs."

"This is California, dear, not the South. We only have scorpions."

"Even worse." I speared a piece of melon with my fork. "What was in there anyway?"

"Boxes of old papers. I put them into a storage unit. We can go through them while we wait for the house to empty."

"If the shed is empty," Morgan said," then why do you think it's worth looking at?"

"Because Kevin built it. I'd bet my new shoes he also put in hidey-type places."

"I'm betting on the boxes in storage." I tore off

a piece of ham and tossed it to Shutterbug who caught it mid-air.

"Maybe," she said, "but Kevin liked to do things a little different. He suspected someone was after him—I see that now—and he would have thought of several ways to keep information safe."

Morgan nodded. "I agree. We'll look everywhere we can."

A knock sounded at the door.

Morgan stood. "Who has a key to the house?"

"Just me, Ruthie, and Brock."

He opened the duffel bag he'd set down and pulled out a Glock. "Be ready to duck if I say down. Come, Shutterbug."

My dog obeyed as if she'd followed his orders all along. She sniffed along the bottom of the door, then sat back and wagged her tail.

Morgan peered out the peephole, then opened the door. "Why didn't you give our special knock?"

Lori brushed past him. "I didn't know you'd arrived yet."

"I rode with Kelly."

She approached the table. "I've found the desk, but it will take a few days to be dug out of storage." She sat across from us at the table, declining my offer to fix her a sandwich. "I have the computer geeks working on decoding your father's file, but I think you and Ruthie are our best bet."

"I bought my old house back," Ruthie said. "We'll search there and in a storage unit I have."

"You bought a house in order to—" She shook her head. "We could have gotten a search warrant."

Ruthie shrugged. "I love that old house. I'll rent

it out and keep it in the family. Maybe someday Kelly will get married and want to live there."

I loved the sprawling ranch house, too, and wasn't opposed to the idea…someday. "Anything on the investigation you can tell us?"

"About the shooter? No, he's a ghost. We didn't find fingerprints on the knife, and no one saw how he got out of the theater." Weariness flickered across her face.

"You still can't trust your fellow officers?"

"I don't know which ones I can, so no. But, there's a couple of new rookies I'm watching. I might be able to get them to help investigate your father's death. They haven't been around long enough to be dirty." She pushed to her feet. "I'll share what I can, but you know I can't tell you everything."

"I know, but you expect me to tell you everything." I bit into my sandwich.

"Unfortunately, that's how it works. Morgan, watch out for these two and keep yourself safe while you're at it."

"You too, sis." He walked her to the door and locked it after her. All of a sudden, he glared out the back windows, then darted outside.

Ruthie and I followed in time to see Morgan scale the back fence. Someone yelled in surprise, then Morgan climbed back.

He grinned sheepishly. "I forgot you had cops patrolling the perimeter."

"I'm shocked that a man your age could scale the fence. How old are you?"

"Sixty." He winked at Ruthie. "I fell for an

older woman."

"Oh, hush. I'm only a few years older and hold my age very well."

"That you do." His eyes smoldered.

Okay. Time for me to leave. I wanted my grandmother to be happy, but I didn't have to watch the gushy stuff.

Brock stood in the living room when I entered and held out his arms. I stepped into them and lifted my face for a kiss feeling safer than I had all day. Yes, Morgan would give his life for me and Ruthie, but the man holding me guarded my heart. "When did you get here?"

"A few seconds ago. I can't stay away long." He rested his chin on my head. "I worried about you all day. I'm glad to see Morgan here."

"I thought it a good idea."

He took my hand and led me to the sofa. "There's something I need to tell you."

"Okay."

"I got my conceal and carry permit today."

Chapter Four

I'd fallen asleep the night before, rattled by the thought of Brock carrying a gun. He'd come a long way from the mostly self-absorbed celebrity he was when we first met. Clueless as to the seedier side of life. Now he met danger head-on and had become a force that I reckoned with. I smiled. My man.

My smile faded as Morgan opened Ruthie's large rented storage unit. Boxes upon boxes lined the walls. Furniture formed unstable towers. "How does one person need so much stuff?"

"Some of this furniture is antique," Ruthie said. "Other pieces hold sentimental memories, and one never knows when they might need a paper in those files." She wagged a finger at me. "If we find what we need in here, you'll be glad I kept them."

True. "This will take the whole week between now and access to the house."

She grinned. "Maybe we won't need to search the house."

She made a lot of sense that morning, which threatened to topple my world on its axis. I sighed and grabbed the first box to shove into the back of the truck we'd rented.

By the time we finished hauling boxes, I was tired and sweaty. I groaned, knowing we had to unload them once we arrived home. I reached for the latch to close the unit when my gaze fell on an antique roll-top desk in the back. A desk that had sat in my father's study for most of my childhood.

I released the door and stumbled through the maze of furniture. Emotions flooded through me as I ran my hands over the oak wood. I could picture my father sitting at this desk paying his bills. He'd locked the checkbook...locked.

I reached for the small drawer on my right. It slid open, not locked as it used to be kept. I hunkered down in front of the desk and ran my hands under, in, and around every nook and cranny. Bingo. The key.

"But you opened the drawer," Ruthie said peering over my shoulder.

I stood. "There's a space hidden behind this drawer." I slid aside a panel the size of an envelope. Reaching inside, I pulled out a sheet of paper. My first poem written when I was seven, an ode to my father.

"I remember that." Ruthie placed a hand on my shoulder. "It won't help us break the code, but you keep it. Don't hide it away again."

"It'll be in a frame on my wall by night time." I

folded it and shoved it in my pocket. There'd be no code in the desk. Dad had stopped using it a couple of years before his death, but the memories were priceless. "I'd like this desk brought to my room, please."

"I'll come back and get it," Morgan said. "I promise."

I nodded and headed for the truck.

By lunchtime, the formal dining room had been converted into a storage unit. Boxes hid the stylish wallpaper and fine art. The task before us seemed formidable. I started to sag onto a cream-colored chair, then glanced down at my dusty clothes and plopped on the floor instead.

"This can wait until tomorrow." Ruth clapped her hands. "Let's go to the beach. We need a break."

That got me to my feet. I sent Brock a text to meet us there and rushed to get my bathing suit.

Brock waited for us in the parking lot of Huntington Beach. Brutus leaped around his feet as Brock grabbed a couple of beach chairs, then the puppy bounded across the sand with Shutterbug. Sassy, being the little princess that she was, peered over the edge of the doggy bag Ruthie carried her in and yipped. Beach time pandemonium. I loved it.

We set up our umbrellas, chairs, ice chests, and beach bags at the edge of where dry sand met damp. I dropped my coverup and ran for the water, diving under an approaching wave.

Nothing relieved stress like the sound of waves lapping the shore, the cry of seagulls, and the feeling of water engulfing you. I let the waves toss me here and there before lodging my feet on the sandy bottom. I brushed the hair from my eyes.

A man stood on the shore, his features shadowed with the sun behind him. He appeared to be staring at me, then turned and headed down the beach.

I glanced behind me, noticing a few people surfing further out. Most likely he'd been watching them. At least I thought so until he stopped to watch Ruthie and Sassy at the water's edge.

Morgan noticed him, too, and casually joined Ruthie and her dog. A few minutes later, they strolled along the beach, Morgan keeping his body between Ruthie and the stranger.

Shutterbug splashed to my side as if she felt the trickle of unease course through me. I rested a reassuring hand on her head and joined Brock and Brutus under the beach umbrella. Wrapping my arms around my bent knees, I stared at the place the stranger had turned and headed back the way he'd come. "That man watched Ruthie and Sassy play in the water."

"What?" Brock set down the pages of script for his movie. "Are you sure?"

"Pretty sure. That's why Morgan joined her at the surf's edge." I can't help but wonder if he's the shooter. The build's the same, but without having seen the man's face before, I can't be sure.

I pushed to my feet and called for Shutterbug. "I'm going to follow him for a while."

"Not without me." Brock sprang to his feet slapped a floppy hat on his head, then slipped on dark sunglasses.

I laughed. "Do you really think that disguise is going to work? You had the umbrella pulled so far down I'm surprised you didn't feel claustrophobic."

He grinned. "I did, kind of. I'd like to enjoy a day at the beach."

"Then you shouldn't be so pretty." I gave him a playful punch in the arm as we strolled down the sand hand-in-hand. We hadn't gone far before someone shouted out Brock's name and a gaggle of young women surrounded us, touching his arms, his chest, until he handed me his hat and glasses and hurried into the water too far for them to follow. Something that didn't make Brutus happy. The poor pup tried to follow but kept getting pushed back by the waves.

I felt sympathy for both man and beast. Gesturing to Brock that I was going to continue my walk, I patted my leg for Brutus to follow. Brock motioned that he would swim in the same direction.

The women jogged down the beach, keeping pace. The downfalls of being a celebrity. I snapped a few photos of Brock without his shirt standing in the water. Candid shots were always good for publicity when sold to tabloids.

The man had stopped, again looking our way. Without being too obvious, I motioned again to Shutterbug to follow, and on the pretense of hunting for shells, made my way closer to the stranger on the beach.

After I'd gone several yards, the group of girls lost interest and headed back to wherever they'd run from. Brock shook the water from his hair and joined me at water's edge. He cast a wary glance over his shoulder, then donned his hat and glasses. "I wish they wouldn't touch me."

I laughed and slipped my hand into his. "I'm not a fan of other women touching you either."

"Don't get too famous. I'll punch any man who lays a hand on you." He bent down and kissed me.

A little farther ahead, the stranger turned and jogged away from us. I shrugged. If he had been watching Ruthie with evil intent, we'd succeeded in running him off. For now.

Ruthie handed us each a sandwich as we sat down. "Don't say a word, I've heard it all from Morgan, and I will not stay locked in my house because of a mad man."

I opened my mouth to retort, then snapped it closed. I'd feel the same in her situation, and since I'd been shot at, I could relate. To keep from saying something to make her mad, I bit into my chicken salad sandwich.

We sat and watched the sunset, Brock's arm across my shoulders as we ignored the camera's taking photo after photo for eager fans and rude paparazzi. Oh, well, I'd been one of those. It felt like a lifetime ago. I rested my head on Brock's shoulder and admired God's handiwork of icing the waves with silver frosting and laying a path of gold across the water.

When it became too dark to see and Morgan repeated for the tenth time that we shouldn't be out after dark, we packed up and trudged across the sand to our vehicles. Tired, sandy, and sunburned, we'd enjoyed a wonderful day.

I showered as soon as we arrived home, then

dressed in my comfiest baggy clothes and stared at the stacks of file boxes in the dining room. We'd agreed to wait until the next day, but the files called my name. The key code was in there somewhere. I'd put money on the fact the boxes held the answer and not the old shed behind Ruthie's former home.

Brock thrust a bowl of vanilla ice cream, drizzled with chocolate, into my hand. "What's going on in that head of yours?"

"Will we know the code when we see it?"

"I hope so." He spooned some ice cream into his mouth. "Otherwise, we'll have wasted a lot of time."

Chapter Five

Using a pair of scissors, I cut through the tape holding the first box closed. Folders containing every sheet of artwork I'd done in elementary school filled the container.

I choked back the tears. To think my papers had been kept all these years because of sentimentality. I set the box aside to go through later and pare down my childhood drawings. After writing school artwork on the side of the box, I turned to the next one in line.

Brock hadn't arrived yet, Ruthie still slept, and Morgan slumbered on the sofa in the other room, leaving me and Shutterbug to start the large task in the quiet of early morning.

Box number two held receipts seemingly tossed in at random. After picking up a few with the date 1995, I set the box in the discard pile. Who in the world kept receipts that old?

"Good morning." Ruthie, clutching Sassy in one arm, shuffled past in the direction of the kitchen. She froze at the sight of Morgan and whirled to stare at me with wide eyes. An avocado mask covered her face. Rollers stuck out around her head like Medusa's snakes. "Why is he sleeping on the sofa?" she hissed.

"Because someone has to get through me to get to you," Morgan mumbled.

"He's awake!" Ruthie gasped and sprinted for her room.

I laughed and pushed to my feet to put on a pot of coffee. My poor vain grandmother couldn't start her day without java, but vanity won out. She wouldn't emerge from her room again until her hair and face were made up to perfection.

As I opened the cookie jar to grab a dog treat for Shutterbug, the sound of heavy paws sounded behind me. I smiled and retrieved a second treat, whirling to see my Brock Handsome lounging in the doorway.

"You've already started work without me."

"I did." I tossed each dog a treat. Shutterbug caught hers in midair, Brutus missed and pushed his around the tiled floor until it stopped against the baseboard. "Only two boxes. There's plenty more for you to go through."

"When you're finished with the furry babies, I could stand a kiss from *my* baby."

He didn't need to ask a second time. I stepped into his arms and tilted my face to his. His kiss started slow, then turned hotter, more demanding, his hands on the low of my back. He pulled away and leaned his forehead against mine. "You, my beautiful lady, are a temptation that gets harder to ignore."

I fought to steady my breathing. "I know the feeling." I stepped back and pulled four coffee mugs from the cabinet.

It might not be the norm in Hollywood, but I'd made a vow a long time ago to wait for marriage. I didn't want to give a piece of myself to any man that didn't want to put a ring on my finger. I set the mugs down and leaned on the counter. But then, I hadn't known Brock back then. Talk about temptation.

He stepped behind me and wrapped his arms around my waist. I leaned back into him, breathing in the scent of sea hair and musky cologne.

With a sigh, I straightened and poured our coffee, handing him one and carrying one to Morgan. The old man groaned and sat up.

"This is the most uncomfortable sofa to sleep on."

"You were offered a guest room."

He shook his head. "Nope, I need to be here where an intruder can gain access."

I shrugged. "Then you can't complain."

"Yes, I can," he said with a grin, "but it will obviously do no good. You're a hard-hearted woman, Canyon."

I laughed, flashed a grin at Brock, then sat cross-legged on the dining room floor to return to work.

Brock sat a few boxes down from me. "Am I culling or just searching?"

"If it looks like junk, set it aside and I'll go through it with Ruthie." Childhood memories were not junk, but old receipts were. Where was that code key? My eyes surveyed the twenty or so boxes. It had to be here. If we struck out here and at the house, I had no idea where to go next.

I also couldn't spend too much time finding the key. Ruthie's life was still in danger. Maybe locating the shooter would also help us locate the dirty cops my father tried to expose.

"What are you thinking?" Brock interrupted my musing. "You've stared at that box for several minutes without opening it."

"What if we never find it?" I swallowed past the lump in my throat.

"We will."

"We might not."

"Maybe not today, tomorrow, or even next week, Kelly, but we will solve your father's murder and put away his killer, with or without breaking the code." He gave me a lopsided smile. "Think of the book you could write about it all."

"It's not all about the book, Brock!" I lunged to my feet. "My father's death needs solving, that poor maintenance man's death needs justice, and we need to catch the man who tried to shoot me and Ruthie."

He stood and gathered me in his arms. "I understand your need to solve these crimes is because your father's case remains unsolved. I'm helping in any way I can."

"I know." I rested my cheek against his shoulder and let the safety of his hold calm me before I turned back to open another box.

Within the hour, Ruthie and Morgan joined us. None of us spoke, the dogs playing and the rustle of papers the only sounds in the room until Ruthie slapped the top of a box.

"I've been thinking and I don't need any smart comments about my doing so," she said glancing at me, "but my son liked to play games. I'm starting to believe that the key to all this will be located with clues."

"Like a scavenger hunt?" Brock stared at her.

She nodded. "What better way to keep those who shouldn't find the information from discovering it?"

I sat back on my thighs and thought. Dad used to draw me pictures of animals on the napkins he tucked into my lunchbox. Each animal stood for the first letter of the animal's name. We'd started this after someone saw his 'I love you' and teased me.

"Find every box with childish drawings," I said, pulling the box I'd opened first toward me. "I think Ruthie is on to something."

I pulled every piece of paper that wasn't drawn by my childish hand. Soon twenty pages lay in front of me. "Thank you, Dad." He'd numbered the pages. Once I arranged them in numerical order, I swept them into my hands and moved to the table. "Give me a few minutes and I'll know what our next step is."

I worked in a frenzy for over an hour, drinking my coffee out of habit and nibbling on toast. The others sat across from me and watched, thankfully keeping silent so I could work.

"I've got it, or at least the next step." I flipped around the page I'd written on so they could see the words.

"Go to the place it all began," Brock read before meeting my gaze. "Where's that?"

"My house," Ruthie said. "Kevin grew up there."

"So, we search the old house just to find the next step?" Morgan crossed his arms. "You don't think this is a wild goose chase?"

"No, I don't." I stood and put the pages in a pile. "I'm going to shred the page that tells us the next step and put these others back in the box."

"Good idea." Ruthie pushed to her feet. "We'll head to the house first thing after breakfast."

"Do you have blueprints of the house?" Brock glanced from me to Ruthie. "That would let us know if there are walls that weren't there when the house was built."

Ruthie grinned. "You're more than a pretty face, Brock. Excellent! I'll call the courthouse and see if I can have them delivered today. Why don't the rest of you sit out by the pool? I'll fix lunch and bring it out. We've earned some relaxation. You'll find men's trunks in assorted sizes in the bathhouse."

I didn't need to be told twice. I made a dash to my room and donned my suit, wrapping a matching sarong around my waist. It might be my home, but I wasn't going to parade around in nothing but the suit in front of Morgan. The man was a workout fiend, and Brock spent a lot of time at the gym.

Shutterbug leaned her paws on the windowsill and growled low in her throat. The hair along her back bristled.

I caught a glimpse of a pair of eyes staring through a slit in the blinds and screamed.

Chapter six

Once I overcame the shock of a Peeping Tom, I ordered Shutterbug to "get him," and raced down the hall and outside after her. Morgan and Brock didn't ask questions, followed, although Morgan clutched his gun in his hand and yelled for Ruthie to stay in the house and lock the door.

The men soon overtook me and positioned themselves between me and the running peeper. Ignoring their demands to go stay with Ruthie, I thundered after them.

Shutterbug gave three sharp barks. Her signal that she'd cornered something. When we caught up to her, a man in dirty, ragged clothing peered down from the branches of a tree.

"Get your butt down here," Morgan ordered, aiming his weapon. "Now."

"Call off the dog."

I snapped my fingers and motioned for

Shutterbug to sit next to me. "Any funny moves and I'll sic her on you."

The man paled, but swung down out of the tree. "I just wanted something to eat."

"From the back of the office?" Morgan shoved the man in the direction we'd run. "You'll be coming with us and answering some questions."

The man eyed Shutterbug and nodded. "Sure thing, dude."

Brock walked between me and "Tom," taking my hand in his. "You shouldn't run after people who may intend you harm."

I squeezed his hand. "Pure reflex." I grinned up at him. "Besides, Shutterbug had everything under control."

He frowned. "Call me or Morgan next time, please."

"I thought that's what my scream was for."

Ruthie opened the front door as we approached. "What happened? You three took off out of here with nothing but warnings. I've been worried sick."

Morgan patted her cheek. "It's fine, sweetheart."

"No, it isn't," our captive said. "I'm starving and dying of thirst. Have pity, lady."

Brock, Morgan, and I gave a collective sigh. Ruthie could never turn down someone who was hungry.

"You come right in, young man, and we'll remedy that." She stepped back so we could enter.

"Not until we question him," Morgan said, motioning the man toward a kitchen chair. "Let's start with your name."

I told Shutterbug to sit close to our unwanted guest and keep her eyes on him. She sat close enough that the man had to feel her breath on his leg.

"Dan Jones."

"Why were you looking in this woman's window? From the backyard?"

Dan glanced from Morgan to me. "I was paid to watch you all. You really need a higher fence. I didn't have any trouble scaling it." He winked at me. "You're a real looker. It wasn't a hardship peeping in on a movie star."

I kicked his shin, then hopped as my toe connected with bone. "Search him. I don't want any nude pictures of me showing up on social media."

Brock patted the man down and pulled out a disposable camera. "Paid you, my foot. You were hoping to sell photos to make money. Am I right?"

He shrugged. "Can't blame a guy for trying."

"Actually, we can," Morgan said. "Taking photos of someone unaware and trespassing are against the law."

"Are you calling the cops?" He started to stand.

Morgan pushed him back down. "Maybe."

"I'll tell you whatever you want to know. Yes, someone paid me to watch you, yes, I hoped to sell pictures for money over and above that, and no, I'm not a danger to anyone…just homeless. Selling those pictures would have rented me a place for a good long while."

Pity tugged at my heart. I continued to hope that America's homeless would be taken care of, but I wasn't willing to go so far as to allow a man to peep at me and take pictures. "Give me the phone. I want to check the pictures."

Thankfully, Brock nor Morgan hadn't looked at the photos. I flipped through them. "These are pretty good, despite the cheap camera." I tossed it in the garbage, then scribbled the number and contact person for the *Hollywood Tribune* on a scrap of paper. "I used to work here. Tell them I said to hire you." I narrowed my eyes. "If you really do want to better your life."

"Oh, I do. Thanks." He shoved the slip of paper into his pocket. "I'm not one of them drunks or druggies. Just down on my luck."

"It's all freelance, Dan. You'll have to get out there and take photos good enough to sell without breaking the law to get them."

Morgan made a disgusted noise in his throat. "Stop mollycoddling the man. I want to know who hired you."

"I don't know who it was. A man in a hoodie came up to me in an alley and handed me twenty dollars and this phone. Said to take pictures of what you guys were up to. What's in all those boxes?"

"None of your business. What did this man look like? White? Black? Short…"

"Big. Close to your size. I couldn't see his face because he had the hood pulled low, but his hands were those of a white man. He had a deep voice." Dan rubbed his chin. "He talked like a cop. You know, all authoritative and stuff."

Morgan glanced at me. "Call Lori."

I nodded and stepped into the kitchen. Shaking my head at the amount of food piled on a plate for

Dan to eat, I dialed Lori's number.

"Detective Lawrence."

"It's Kelly. Morgan told me to call you. We caught a Peeping Tom who said someone hired him to watch us. He thinks it might have been a cop."

"I'll be there in twenty minutes." Click.

"Stop harassing that man and let him eat." Ruthie set the food and a glass of water on the kitchen table. "You can talk more when Lori gets here."

"Who's Lori?" Dan sat at the table, his eyes wide. "I'll never be able to eat all this." A large chicken breast, broccoli, mashed potatoes, and two rolls with butter covered his plate.

"Then you can take it with you." Ruthie patted his shoulder. "Eat."

Morgan muttered something about kindhearted women, then moved back to the front room to wait for his sister. He didn't have to wait longer than the promised twenty minutes. One minute after entering the house, Lori sat across from Dan.

"I'm Detective Lawrence."

"Hey!" He glared at Morgan. "I thought you weren't going to have me arrested."

"That all depends on you, sir." Lori straightened. "Tell me everything you just told Mr. Lawrence." She motioned her head at Morgan. "Cooperation will work in your favor."

He repeated everything he'd told us, then resumed eating. "I don't know anything else."

"You said you thought he was a cop."

"Yep. He talked like one. Short sentences, clipped words, harsh tone."

"Would you recognize his voice if you heard it again?"

"I doubt it. He spoke low. I had to listen carefully to hear over the sound of all the cars going by. Are we finished? I have to go get cleaned up and rent me a camera." He pushed to his feet. "Thanks for the food, ma'am." He nodded at Ruthie.

Rent a camera? Steal would be more like it. Where would a homeless person get enough money to purchase the type of camera he needed to take photos worthy of selling? I almost offered him my old Kodak but didn't want him to sell it for cash. No, he'd have to figure it out on his own.

Morgan escorted Dan to the front door. "If I see you around here again, I'll shoot you."

Dan paled. "Got it." He couldn't get out the door fast enough when Shutterbug rushed toward him.

My sweet girl. I patted her head. "Ferocious beast."

Morgan laughed. "That she is. Would she have hurt him?"

"No, not unless he was a physical threat to me, but that's our little secret." I sat next to Lori. "Now what? How does this relate to my father's death and the poor maintenance man's? Are they even connected?"

"His name was Roy Little, and yes, I think they're connected. I just don't know how yet."

Chapter seven

The next morning, I stood in the backyard where I'd spent most of my childhood and stared at the white painted boards of the storage shed. The previous owner, as asked, had left the building untouched, giving Ruthie the time to retrieve the items inside. How could people have so much stuff to have to rent storage units, fill garages, and have a separate building to house their possessions?

Ruthie unlocked the padlock and swung the doors open, which shrieked on rusty hinges to reveal another horde of boxes. I sighed and stepped inside, reaching above my head to pull the chain of the single lightbulb overhead.

"I was a little more organized here," Ruthie said. "I'd taken a break from my career and had more free time. These boxes are all labeled, in great detail, on the sides." She grinned.

Brock rubbed his hands together. "Great. This

will make the job easier."

I navigated the narrow aisle between the boxes, reading what was written in black marker on the sides. Toys, baby clothes, blankets, receipts…more receipts, clothes, etc. Everything that should have been thrown away and wasn't. I grabbed a box marked important papers and carried it outside to the patio table.

Wrapped with a faded pink ribbon were letters from my mother to my father when he'd gone to the police academy. She'd died of cancer soon after his return. I understood the need to save such valuable letters and set them aside to go through later.

Forty-five minutes passed, and I hadn't found anything that looked remotely like another message from my father. "Anyone finding anything?"

"Nothing." Morgan glanced at the house. "Anything in there?"

Ruthie shook her head. "I moved everything out when I sold the place."

Brock paced the yard mumbling and doing his best not to trip over Brutus who chased Sassy in and out of our feet. "Wait a minute." His gaze met mine. "Your father's message said to start where it all began."

"My baby stuff." I darted back into the shed, Brock on my heels. We grabbed every box that had to do with my childhood and set them on the patio table.

Inside my jewelry box was a small folded piece of paper the size of a business card. Written on it was one word, "Harvey."

"Who's Harvey?" Morgan asked. "Your father

sure wasn't taking any chances of anyone finding out what he was on to."

I knew exactly who Harvey was. A chipped cement angel poured water from an urn into the pool. As an only child, there were times loneliness filled me and I'd made the angel a silent friend. "This is Harvey." I put a hand on the angel that stood on top of a cement box that put him face-to-face with me.

Trailing my fingers along my friend, I searched for a place Dad could have left us another message. A small hole in the back of Harvey's head held a key. I pulled it out and held it up.

"That looks like a safety deposit box key," Brock said. "Ruthie?"

"I don't know anything about Kevin having a safety deposit box, but we can check the nearby banks."

I sagged against Harvey, dropping the key into my pocket. "One more thing that might, or might not, make this all clear to us." Just how close had my father come to discovering who was the dirty cop? Someone killed my father for what he knew, which led me to believe he had been very close to revealing the identity of whichever cop or cops were taking protection payments.

"Let's look at this differently." Morgan sat in one of the patio chairs. "Who would need the protection?"

"Important people," I said, sitting across from him.

"Exactly. Who in our close circle seems to always be in trouble and short on cash?"

"William Johnson, Junior?" I frowned. "He got shot the last time he acted up. Do you think whoever shot him did so because he wouldn't pay?"

Morgan shrugged. "People have been shot for less. Did your father know Johnson?"

"Of course he did," Ruthie said. "He was an actor for a while before turning to law enforcement. Everyone in the business knows the studio owners are as crooked as writhing snakes."

The back gate squeaked.

We turned.

Two masked men holding guns stepped around the corner of the house and aimed their weapons at us. "Sit down."

Those of us who were still standing complied with his request.

The one who'd ordered us to sit pulled Morgan's gun from his waistband. The other man kept his gun trained on me and didn't say a word. Something about him struck me as familiar.

"Do I know you?"

He didn't flinch or answer.

"No talking," the other one said, "unless you're asked a question. So, pretty little gal, what are you looking for?"

"Memorabilia." I motioned at my childish treasures. "We're going to rent the house, and I wanted to go through the shed before we did."

"You're lying. Our informant told us you had lots of boxes piled up in your house and papers scattered around. What did you find?" He fired at my feet, kicking up a piece of flagstone.

"Bills, receipts…what do you expect us to

find?" I tucked my feet under me and tried not to flinch as I kept my gaze locked on his. I was going to kill Dan, the little sneak.

"Your father stuck his nose where it didn't belong, and if you don't stop, Canyon, you'll suffer the same fate. You won't get another warning." The two turned and sprinted away.

"Who's paying you?" I shouted after them.

The only answer I got was the slamming of the iron gate and the pounding of Morgan's feet as he gave chase.

Brock stuck close to my side. "He shouldn't go. They took his weapon."

"Where's your gun?"

"In the car." He sighed. "I've got to get used to carrying it, I guess."

"If you're going to keep hanging around me, you will."

Morgan returned a few minutes later. "They got away with my gun. I loved that gun. I'm calling Lori. She's going to think I can't do my job."

"She won't think that," Ruthie said, patting his cheek. "She'll understand that they stole it and you're still standing here breathing without a new hole in your body."

He gave Ruthie a tender smile and turned away to call his sister.

"Now what?" She asked me.

"We find out what's in that safety deposit box."

"I'll start making some calls and see if I can find out which bank." She left and disappeared into the house, calling for Sassy to follow her. When the dog didn't appear, I noticed Brutus and Shutterbug were also gone. That's why the masked men had been able to catch us off guard.

I dashed around the corner of the house. The gate had bounced open. Just outside of it lay the three dogs. Shutterbug had a tranquilizer dart in her shoulder. All three were unconscious.

"Brock! Morgan!" I dropped to my knees and put my hands on Shutterbug's stomach. She still breathed.

Brock scooped her into his arms, leaving me to carry Brutus, who didn't weigh much less. Ruthie tucked Sassy under her chin and we sprinted for the car, Morgan on her heels.

Several hours later, after finding out our fur babies would be fine after the sedative wore off, we met Lori, not at the old house, but the new.

"Where was Warren today?" I asked her.

"Why?" She narrowed her eyes.

"Because one of the men seemed familiar to me and matched the description of the masked man who hired Dan. Warren also fits that description."

"He went with me to a domestic dispute, then said the new chief-of-police needed to see him. He was gone for a couple of hours, but he's at the station now."

"Enough time for him to confront us?"

She nodded. "Probably. If he's on to you—"

I leaned forward. "You do think he's dirty."

"Not just him. He isn't smart enough to be at the head of this. We find the one in charge, and we can shut this down." She pulled a Glock from her leather bag and handed it to her brother.

Morgan grinned. "Thanks."

"You can't protect these people without one." She pushed to her feet. "Maybe the four of you should go away for a while."

"I can't," Brock said. "I'm in the middle of a film."

"We start filming early next week," I added. "We'll have to keep our eyes open and continue on as we have been."

She sighed. "Try to stay alive, would you? If something happens to you, your father will come back to haunt me." The sad smile she gave led me to believe that might not be a bad thing to her.

"They won't catch me by surprise again, sis." Morgan tucked the gun into his waistband. "Even when I think we're safe, I'll have it where I can grab it easily."

"Don't die on me, brother. You're the only one I've got." She flashed a grin and left via the front door.

Shutterbug nudged my hand and tears trailed down my cheeks.

"You care more about her than you do yourself," Morgan said.

"Yes, I do." I knelt and nuzzled her neck. "Next to Brock and Ruthie—and you, too, I guess, she's the most important thing to me."

Brock laughed. "At least she included me."

I reached up and clasped his hand. "Of course, you're Brock Handsome."

Chapter Eight

The safety deposit box contained another key. One I recognized. This key belonged to a locker at the bus station. Once, when Dad took me on a day trip along Pacific Coast Highway, he insisted we take the bus as it was an experience everyone should enjoy. We'd stowed a few items in the locker for spending a couple of hours at the beach when we returned later in the day.

So, we made our way to the bus station and headed to locker 107. We were coming to the end of solving this, I just knew it.

Inside the locker was an empty duffel. My shoulders sagged. Maybe Dad hadn't had time to fill it with the information he wanted me to find.

Brock rested a consoling hand on my shoulder. "We'll figure it out, sweetheart."

"Let's take a break from this," Morgan said, "and concentrate on the dead janitor. Lori seems to think the two are related. Maybe…if we solve that mystery, we'll figure out your father's riddle."

"Okay." I blinked back tears and shuffled back to the car. Once I'd taken my seat, I ran over in my head what we knew of the award's night and the murder of Roy Little. Weapon, screw driver. Uniform stolen. Killer tried to shoot Ruthie, then trained the gun on me. Which meant my grandmother knows something she doesn't know she knows. How could we access the information from inside her head to help us?

"Let's go back to the award venue. It's still a crime scene. Maybe we'll see something everyone missed." I clicked my seatbelt into place.

Morgan was right. We find Roy's killer and we might, just might, discover what Dad wanted us to find.

"Stop at the coffee shop," Ruthie said. "I can't continue on without caffeine."

Brock glanced in the rearview mirror. "You had two cups before we left the house."

"Your point?"

Brock stopped and went through the drive-through, ordering everyone's favorite drink. I wanted Shutterbug to have her cream, but four adults filled up the Thunderbird leaving no room for four-legged babies.

Java in hand, we stood at the back of the large building. I cast a glance back and forth, having learned from experience, that crossing under crime scene tape was a big no-no. Hopefully, if caught, having a detective's brother with us would lessen the lecture we'd receive.

Morgan picked the lock on the back door, another no-no, then held it open for the rest of us to enter before closing it. A few seconds later, he lit up the long hallway with the beam of his flashlight.

I clicked on mine and took Brock's hand. "I don't want to explore alone."

His eyes twinkled. "Do I look like the type of man who wouldn't enjoy being in the dark with you?"

I gave a nervous laugh. "Let's all start where I found Roy's body, then spread out."

"Yes, boss." Morgan threw a sharp salute.

I rolled my eyes and led the way.

Roy's blood still stained the floor in the center of the chalk outline of his body. I shuddered, but squatted next to where he'd lain and tried to see things from his point of view.

Had he argued with his killer? Tried to defend himself?

To my right lay his open toolbox next to a box of electrical cables. Had his killer surprised him, stabbing Roy when he turned around? I still thought his death was one of convenience. Until I'd come along wanting more light for taking pictures.

I racked my brain to discern the features of the man I'd convinced to help me turn up the lights. All I knew was that he was Caucasian. Not much help.

Pushing to my feet, I headed down the hall and took the steps to the balcony where the shooter had stood. Morgan and Ruthie headed for the stage. Brock followed me.

From the balcony, with the help of my flashlight, I had a clear view of Morgan and Ruthie.

My grandmother positioned herself where she'd stood that night. I reached over and clutched Brock's hand. "Thank you for tackling Ruthie to the floor."

He raised my hand to his lips and placed a soft kiss on its back. "I'd jump between you two and a bullet anytime."

My Mr. Handsome had come a long way in the last few months. He not only acted as an action hero in the movies, he did so in real life.

The shape of a man rose behind Brock. Before I could utter a warning, he slammed the butt of a pistol across the back of Brock's head, then aimed the weapon at me as Brock crumbled to the floor.

I clicked off my flashlight and ran. Concern for Brock caught my breath, but if my pursuer had wanted him dead, he would've killed him. No, it was me and Ruthie this man wanted.

Footsteps thundered behind me. From the floor below were the heavy thuds of Morgan giving chase and his yells for Ruthie to find a place to hide.

I located the stairs in the dark and dashed down them. My soft-soled canvas shoes made little noise. At the bottom, I dove under a row of seats and froze. Hopefully, the man chasing me wouldn't turn on a light for fear of Morgan finding him. Without light, it would take my pursuer a while to find under which of the hundred rows of seats I'd taken cover. I prayed Morgan would find him before the man found me.

I clasped my hand over my mouth to silence my panting. My eyes strained to see, my ears to hear. The scuff of a nearby shoe caused me to hold my breath.

What were we supposed to know? Everything in me wanted to pop out and demand the shooter tell us what it was he wanted. Common sense urged me to stay put. I'd have trouble figuring out anything if I was dead.

A gunshot rang out. Then another. Someone grabbed me by the ankle and yanked me from my hiding place, then against a solid chest, his hand over my mouth.

"Shh." Brock whispered, pulling me into an alcove.

I nodded and removed his hand. My eyes had adjusted some to the darkness and I saw the figure of a man dart in front of where we stood. I couldn't tell if it was Morgan or the other man.

A few tense minutes later, Morgan called for us to come out. "He's gone. Ruthie?"

"Here," she said from the direction of the stage.

He shined his light, illuminating the spot where she rose to her feet from behind the podium. "That wasn't the best place to hide, sweetheart."

"No, but it was a fast place to hide."

I laughed and leaned into Brock. "How did you know where I was?"

"I thought of where an itty-bitty thing like you could squeeze and went from there."

I flipped on my flashlight and shined it on his face. "You're bleeding."

"I took quite a whack to the back of the head, remember?" His mouth crooked.

"He knew we were here. He followed us," I said when the other two joined us."

Morgan gave a sharp nod. "We need to check the house for bugs."

While I tended to Brock's head back at the house, Morgan searched for listening devices. He flipped chairs, turned on lights, and studied every corner.

"Does it hurt much?" I dabbed a wet cloth to the back of Brock's head.

"A bit. Does it need stitches?"

"I don't think so. The bleeding has almost stopped." I set the rag down and poured three ibuprofen tablets into the palm of my hand, handing them and a glass of water to Brock. "These might help." I sagged into the chair next to him. "I was so scared when he hit you and you fell."

"No more than I was when I woke up and you were gone." He popped the pills into his mouth and took a gulp of the water.

Morgan joined us and held out his hand. Tiny silver circles that resembled watch batteries lay in his palm. "One in every room."

My eyes widened. "The person on the other end of these knows everything we've said and planned."

The doorbell rang, sending all three dogs into a barking frenzy. Well, Buster's was more of a low woof, since Mastiffs weren't big barkers. Still, the person on the other side of the door was aware we had dogs.

Morgan dropped the bugs on the table. "Put those in a soundproof box and call Lori." He opened the front door as I unlocked a safe behind the oil painting on the wall and put the bugs inside.

"Delivery for Ruthie Canyon." A young man wearing a bicycle helmet held out a box.

Morgan took the box and slammed the door. "Ruthie?"

"You should have tipped the poor boy," she said, exiting the kitchen.

"Did you order something?"

"I did the moment we got home." She took the box from him and set it on the table. Using a pair of scissors, she'd carried with her, she slit the tape on the top. After opening the box, she handed each of us a pair of night-vision goggles. "If we would have had these, that man would never have taken us by surprise."

I bit my lip to keep from laughing. Morgan wasn't quite so composed. He threw his head back in laughter, then pulled my grandmother to his side.

"You are the funniest woman I've ever met."

She frowned. "Why? These make perfect sense to me. Next time we go where it's dark, we'll be able to see." She stepped away from him and crossed her arms. "I really don't see what's so funny."

Brock chuckled, then cut it short and winced. "Don't make me laugh. It hurts my head."

"Then don't." Ruthie cut him a sharp glance. "I shouldn't waste my time with you three." With a flounce of her head, she stomped back to the kitchen.

With an amused glance at us, Morgan followed.

"Ruthie always has an answer to everything,

doesn't she?" Brock moved to the sofa and leaned his head back against a folded, crocheted afghan.

"She thinks she does." I dropped down next to him. "We didn't find out anything."

He tilted his head. "Yes, we did. We found out we were being listened to. My guess? Someone got to the bus locker before us and cleaned it out. Why would your father put an empty duffel back inside the locker?"

"You're much more than just a pretty face. You're brilliant, too." I grinned and jumped to my feet. "We figure out what might have been there, and we'll—" I stopped. "The killer thinks we've already seen what was in there."

Brock grinned. "Which means it had to be the very thing we were looking for."

"Which means," I grinned back, "we find whatever that is and we find Dad's killer. I hope Lori has some great ideas on how to go about finding…whatever it is."

Chapter Nine

Lori, along with a man I'd never met and Detective Warren, rang the doorbell a short while later. "This is our new chief-of-police, Mr. Warren Foster."

The look in Lori's eyes told me she didn't trust the man and to tread softly. "It's nice to meet you, sir. Please come in."

Morgan seemed to read his sister's face as easily as I did and, instead of asking questions, stuck out his hand. "I'm Morgan Lawrence."

The chief's gaze moved from Morgan to Lori. "Related?"

"Yes sir, Morgan is my brother. That's why I asked him to be bodyguard to the Canyons." The stiffness in Lori's shoulders showed her irritation at not being able to arrive alone.

"Come on in," Ruthie said. "I've put coffee on."

The three law enforcement officers sat at the

kitchen table. Chief Foster spoke first. "You were attacked at the theater?"

I nodded. "Brock was injured. Morgan ran the perpetrator off."

His gaze hardened. "Your father was a cop, Miss Canyon. You are not. Please do not act as if you are."

"By saying perpetrator?" I crossed my arms. "That's what the man would be called, right?"

His face darkened. "Detective Warren has filled me in on your meddling in this murder investigation. I'm telling you to stop or I'll drag you to jail." He pushed to his feet. "Detective Lawrence, you are too close to this case. I'm removing you and placing you on administrative leave, with pay until this case is solved." He gave a definitive nod and strode out the front door with Warren in his wake.

I turned to Lori. "What just happened?"

"Something good if you stop and think about it. Now I don't have to tiptoe around either one of them." She smiled. "Tell me what you found?"

Still shocked by what had just transpired, I recounted our dash through the theater, the empty duffle bag, and the retrieved listening devices. "We think whatever was in the locker was stolen before we arrived."

"I agree." She took a deep breath. "Who would have the most to lose by you getting there first? The cop Kevin was after?"

"You don't trust the new chief, why?" I leaned my elbows on the table.

Frown lines formed on her forehead. "A gut feeling. Nothing I can put my finger on, but his putting me on leave strengthens that feeling.”

“Won’t your continuing to investigate put you in trouble?” Morgan asked.

“Most definitely, but I’m resolved to get to the bottom of this. I’ve some files at my house pertaining to Little’s death. I’ll go retrieve them and bring them back here. There has to be something we’ve missed.”

“We can follow you.” I suggested.

She shook her head. “I haven’t checked my place for bugs. Until I do, this is our safest place to plan our attack.”

After she left, Morgan turned to me. “I don’t like this. Her insistence on continuing puts a huge target on her back. Especially if Foster or Warren are dirty.”

“We keep coming up against brick walls.” I slapped my palm flat on the tabletop. “I’m clueless right now.”

Brock, who had remained silent, spoke up. “Your father seems to have been a careful man. He would have anticipated something like this happening. I think he would have made a backup plan.”

“Copies of what was in the locker. Of course.” I shot to my feet. Where would he have stashed the copies?

Ruthie brought four mugs of coffee on a silver tray and set it in the center of the table. “Remember my family home on the beach?”

“Doesn’t someone live there?” I whirled to face her.

“Not in a year. I need to have some repairs

done, or sell it, but I haven't had the time to do either."

I couldn't remember for sure the last time we'd been to the house in Venice but guessed I'd been around twelve. Dad didn't like my young eyes darting around Muscle Beach. "Did Dad spend much time there?"

"Before we started renting it, he would go there when he needed to clear his mind. I didn't bring it up because the clues we found so clearly led us in a different direction. If we go searching, it will also give me the opportunity to see what needs fixing."

"We'll go as soon as Lori gets back." I moved to peer out the back-glass doors.

A man in a dark ski mask leaped over the fence. His eyes widened when he caught sight of me. Before he could jump over, I opened the door and let Shutterbug loose.

"Get 'em."

"You too, Sassy." Ruthie pointed. "Get that bad man."

Brutus lumbered after the other two. The Mastiff might be a puppy, but his size would deter anyone.

The masked intruder tried scaling the wall only to have Sassy latch onto his pant leg. He flung her off and lost his grip, landing flat on his back. Shutterbug stood over him and growled.

I knew before yanking off the mask that we'd caught Dan the Peeping Tom once again. "What is it this time?" I tossed the mask at Brock.

"Same thing," he said, not taking his eyes off my dog. "Watch you and relay any information. The guy paid me five hundred dollars."

"I offered you the opportunity to get an honest job, Dan."

"I did. You can't blame me for taking the opportunity to make a little more cash."

"I can, and as soon as Officer Lawrence arrives, you'll be hauled off to jail. You don't get a second chance with me."

Morgan yanked the young man to his feet. "I ought to shoot you and save the taxpayers' money."

"No, no, I'm sorry."

Morgan dragged him into the house and pushed him roughly into a chair. "Watch him, Shutterbug."

All three of the dogs fixed their stares on Dan. Sassy didn't last long. Soon she darted to the kitchen in search of something more interesting. The other two sat like statues.

I stood behind them. "You still want us to believe you don't know who hired you?"

"Yep." Dan paled.

The man lied. I bent over and positioned my face inches from his. "I'd be more scared of me siccing those dogs on you than the man who hired you."

"He'll kill me."

"My dogs will tear you apart before you die." I seriously doubted a single word of my threat. Shutterbug acted tough, but she'd never kill. Of that I was certain. But Dan didn't know her like I did.

"All I know is that he's a cop."

"How do you know that? Did you see his face?"

Dan shook his head. "The last call he made to me…I could hear the police radio in the background."

"Did you hear the responding number?" Morgan asked.

"No, I wasn't listening that hard. Seriously, guys, I only wanted the money."

Morgan took my place as interrogator. "This is what we're going to do. You are going to go back to whatever hole you crawled from and tell this cop that we're looking for a list of names. He'll know what we mean. You'll also tell him that we suspect what names are on that list. You'll tell him you overheard all this. Not one mention of us catching you or it will be me you have to worry about. Got it?"

"Got it. Can I go?"

"Yeah." Morgan stepped back.

Dan raced from the house as if his rear end was on fire.

"Why did you tell him we knew the names on the list?" I frowned.

Morgan's grin lacked humor. "Because it's time to draw the rats into a trap."

Chapter Ten

I stood in front of my great grandparents' beach house and wondered when we would have time to set Morgan's trap. Ruthie and I received the call from Louie that we were due back at the studio in the morning to begin filming the next season of our crime drama. That wouldn't leave a lot of time for investigating.

Today would be filled with searching for copies of something we weren't even sure existed. Acting on nothing more than a hunch, we stood to be very disappointed. Again.

"Come on, sweetheart." Brock put his hand on the small of my back. "Let's find those papers, then I'm taking you to dinner."

"That sounds wonderful." I managed a smile. "You are obviously expecting this to take all day."

"Yep." He took a deep breath and opened the bright blue door leading into the house's foyer.

Directly across from the front door were wall-to-wall windows showcasing the beach. A small trail led from the hill the house sat on to the water's edge.

The renters had kept the place in good condition, and other than a new paint job on the outside, the house was ready to sell. I really hoped Ruthie wouldn't. "I think I'd like to live here someday," I said more to myself than anyone else.

"It's yours." Ruthie strolled by with Sassy in her arms. "Move in whenever you like."

"And leave you all alone in that mansion you just bought?"

She cast a soft glance at Morgan. "Perhaps I won't be alone for long." She tossed me a wink and headed to a storage building out back.

Ah. A romance developing right under my nose.

"Where do you want to look first?" Brock asked.

"The attic. The entrance is in the master closet." I led the way and pointed to a door over our heads. "Careful when you pull the rope. The ladder tends to slide down pretty fast."

The floorboards creaked under his feet as Brock grabbed the fraying rope and slowly lowered the ladder, then waved his arm. "After you, beautiful lady."

I laughed and climbed into the darkness. A sour odor stung my nostrils. "What is that smell?"

"Smells like death. Probably a dead squirrel. I'll grab some rags to cover our noses."

I felt for the light switch on the wall to my right, then flicked on the light. The lone bulb swinging from a rafter left the corners of the attic in shadow. "This place used to scare me half to death when I was a kid."

"I can see why." Brock shuddered. "Spiders."

"Afraid?" I raised my eyebrows.

"Most definitely."

"I'll protect you." I pressed my hands on my hips and wondered where Dad might have hidden something of importance. It wasn't a secret the beach house belonged to Ruthie, which meant anyone who suspected something of value was hidden here, would be certain to check the attic. Dad would have known that. So, if he wanted to conceal something, which no one but those closest to him could find…I sighed when nothing came to mind.

"Just start opening boxes. I don't have a clue where to start." I pulled an old chest into the light, sneezing as a cloud of dust assaulted my nose.

Inside, wrapped in faded pink tissue paper, nestled my mother's wedding gown in all its puffy sleeves, lace, and pearls. I hoped to modify the dress and wear it to my own wedding someday and cut a quick glance at Brock.

He smiled and hefted a box from the top of a stack. His dark hair stuck up in disarray and dirt smeared his face. He'd never been more attractive to me.

As I shifted my gaze back to the chest in front of me, I noticed a faint trail in the dust on the attic's floor. Something had been dragged from one spot to the next.

I pushed to my feet, followed the trail and

stopped in front of a pile of boxes. The top one had the distinct handprint of someone having recently placed the box there. I peered around the stack. A woman, dead for a few days from the looks of her, stared back with lifeless eyes.

I gasped and staggered back. "Brock. A body."

"A what?"

"A dead—"

An explosion outside shattered the attic window. I screamed and ducked.

Brock thundered toward me, curling his body over mine. From below came the frantic sound of Shutterbug's barking. Morgan cursed. Ruthie gave a scream of outrage.

"Stay down." Brock pressed slowly to his feet and peered out the broken window. "It looks like someone threw a Molotov cocktail at the house. Morgan and your grandmother are in the backyard, and Morgan is searching for something to break the back door with."

The floor under the attic door creaked.

Brock whirled.

I froze.

The ladder shot down. A man's voice cried out.

I crawled over and peered down. The ladder had knocked the man wearing a ski mask unconscious. "Come on." I scurried down the ladder and unlocked the back door before Morgan could shatter the glass. Then I returned to stare down at the stranger as Brock pulled off the mask.

A young black man wearing a red tee shirt lay there with his eyes closed, a goose egg forming on his forehead.

"Who is he?" I glanced at the others.

"Someone intent on harming you," Morgan said. "We were deliberately locked out of the house. The bomb was a diversion to distract us."

Ruthie glanced out the front window and screamed before darting outside. "Shutterbug, watch him." The rest of us raced after her.

A rock had shattered the window of the Thunderbird. Smaller stones littered the hood. The car wasn't destroyed but would require quite a bit of body work.

"I'm going to kill that man." Tears welled in Ruthie's eyes. She rushed back into the house.

I entered first, just in time to see her pull her Taser from her purse and zap the young man just coming awake. "Ruthie!"

"I don't care. I'll zap him again." And she did.

"Stop, darlin'." Morgan pulled her back by the elbows.

"One more time." She took aim, only to have Morgan drag her away. He plopped her onto the blue-and-white striped sofa. "Sit. Stay. Hug your dog, but no more Tasing."

"Fine." She glared at the young man, whose eyes were beginning to open as Sassy leaped onto his chest. "You're going to pay for my car. Search his pockets."

"Grandma…" I shook my head, then turned to our assailant. "Who hired you and who is the dead woman in the attic?"

His dark eyes widened. "I don't know anything about a dead woman. I was paid five hundred dollars to teach you a lesson."

"By whom?"

He eased to a sitting position and gently removed Sassy, not taking his eyes off Shutterbug. "No idea. A man called me."

"He didn't tell you why?"

"Wait a minute." Morgan held up a hand. "There's a dead woman in the attic?"

I nodded. "You might want to call Lori. No wait, she's off the case. Who do we call that we can trust?"

"We'll have to take our chances with 911. Brock, you call 911, I'm filling Lori in." He stepped away and pressed his phone to his ear.

Brock moved to the opposite side of the room. While both men spoke on their phones, their gaze never left me or the young man on the floor.

"Who are you?" I asked.

He grinned. "Someone you don't want to mess with."

"Drop the attitude or I'll sic the woman with the Taser and my dog on you." I crossed my arms to add force to my words. "Let's try again. Who are you? Your real name and your gang name."

His mouth twitched. "Jerard Homes, Homie is my name."

I narrowed my eyes.

"I'm telling the truth. Look, lady. I got paid, I came to do a job. It ain't personal."

"I want that five hundred dollars," Ruthie called from the sofa.

"Not going to happen, lady."

"You talk tough for someone sitting on the floor," I said.

"Can I go now?"

"Nope. I'm pretty sure you're spending some time in jail." I leaned against the wall opposite him.

What was with the five hundred dollars someone kept paying these idiots? Who was the woman in Ruthie's attic? She had to have something to do with all this.

"Ruthie? Could you go see if you recognize the body in the attic?"

"Gross." She wrinkled her nose, but set Sassy on the floor and climbed the ladder. "Yeah," she yelled down, "that's Georgia Myers. Big actress about thirty years ago. Dated your dad for a while when you were little." She rejoined us. "She used to be real pretty before she…well, you know." Ruthie kicked Jerard as she passed on her way to the sofa.

"Lady, you're going to regret your treatment of me," he said, scowling.

"The only thing I regret is not getting to Tase you a couple more times." She stuck her nose in the air and headed to the kitchen.

Soon, a delectable aroma filled the room and the sounds of approaching sirens filled the air. Good. We would soon be rid of the body and the punk.

"I need medical attention," Jerard said, putting a hand to his head. "You need to fix that ladder."

"I'm sure they'll take care of you in jail." I swiveled as Detective Warren and a younger officer entered the house.

"This is Officer Banks," Warren introduced. "He's my new temporary partner and a rookie. Don't give him a hard time."

I widened my eyes and pressed a hand to my

chest. "Me?"

Warren rolled his eyes, then hauled Jerard to his feet. "Cuff him and put him in the car. I'll check out the attic."

Officer Banks drew a sharp breath through his nose. It didn't take a genius to see he wasn't happy to have Warren as his partner. "Let's go, Homie."

"You know him?" I asked.

"Yep. He's a regular." Banks cuffed him and dragged the reluctant youth outside.

Warren joined us again a few minutes later. "She's been there about three days."

"You're a medical examiner now?" I raised my eyebrows.

Ignoring me, he stalked off outside. Through the open door, I could see him conversing with Banks before the younger officer said something into his radio.

"Lori will meet us back at the house," Morgan said. "She advised us not to tell Warren anything more than answers to his questions and to keep even that to a minimum."

I glanced up and met Brock's gaze. Lori did suspect Warren as being dirty. There was no question now. All we had to do was prove his guilt.

Chapter ELEVEN

No longer on the case, officially at least, Lori joined us for dinner since it couldn't be construed as bribery. "Being on suspension has its ups and downs," she said. "I have more freedom without answering to a boss, but I also don't have access to all the records I need."

"Can we trust Banks?" I set a bowl of salad on the table. "Maybe we could tell him everything and use him to go where you can't."

"I'm not sure yet." She reached for a slice of garlic bread. "I'm pretty sure Warren is dirty, but I don't think he's the brains behind it all, no more than Sawyer was a few months ago. He isn't that smart. I think he's the muscle."

"The man hiring the young men to do his nasty work?"

She nodded. "I'm getting close to proving it too."

I sat across from her and spooned salad in the bowl next to my plate of lasagna. "If my father dated Georgia Myers, then he's been searching for these guys for a very long time."

"Because of his work, we are way closer than we would have been. It won't take us thirty years to bring them down. I promise."

I sighed. First Roy Little, then Georgia, and no clue how their deaths were related other than Dad. "I still don't see how Roy is related to all this."

"Wrong place at the wrong time. The only help in finding his killer is stepping closer to solving this case."

We held hands as Morgan said grace, something new we'd started a few months ago. I rather liked it. With the danger I seemed to get myself into, it didn't hurt to have God on my side.

"Any news on our theater stranger?" Morgan asked while breaking off a piece of garlic bread

"Not a thing." Lori shrugged. "He's like a ghost. A professional hired killer."

"They're expensive, aren't they?" I glanced around the table. "We need to look at someone with money to burn, right?"

"Maybe." Lori cut into her lasagna. "This town is full of people with money."

"Could we be looking at someone in the movie industry?" Morgan pushed his empty salad bowl away and grabbed two more slices of bread.

Lori cocked her head. "I hadn't considered that. Could it be as simple as we're looking in the wrong place?"

"Kevin did spend some time in the industry

before becoming a cop," Ruthie said. "What if he became a police officer because he wanted to stop the corruption?"

"So…" I waved my fork. "We might be looking for someone in the industry with ties to the police force, more specifically someone needing protection for their illegal practices." I suspected William Johnson, the head of the studio, but couldn't fathom he'd be corrupt after the escapades and murder of his son a few months back. Unless… "Could Johnson Junior's drug addiction and murder be what Johnson Senior needs covered up?"

Everyone froze. Silence filled the room. I smiled. I'd hit on a strong possibility. "I guess we start asking questions around the lot tomorrow."

Our first day of filming couldn't have gone worse. Ruthie seemed more focused on telling everyone about our adventure the day before and about finding Georgia's body than she was on remembering her lines.

Louie gave up, giving everyone a two-hour lunch. "Have your heads on straight when you come back," then he muttered something about actors being a bane to society before stalking out of the building.

Great. I had time to question people, and made a beeline for the cafeteria and Mary, the very talkative custodian. I found her emptying garbage cans in preparation for the lunch crowd.

She smiled as I approached. "Welcome back,

Kelly and sweet Shutterbug." She patted my dog's head.

"Thanks. I'm hoping you have time for a few questions."

"Another mystery?"

"Of course." I laughed.

"Sure, if you want to follow me around." She put a fresh bag in the can.

"Is William Johnson, Senior, involved in anything shady? Maybe illegal?"

She frowned. "You sure like to enter dangerous territory, don't you? Now mind you, this is all hearsay. I don't know the man personally, but some folks have said that in the past he required certain…acts from pretty girls before signing them to acting contracts. That was back when he was an agent and not the owner."

"Was Georgia Myers one of those women?"

She flinched. "How did you figure that one out?"

"Lucky guess. That was thirty years ago. What might he be involved in now?"

She grabbed my arm and pulled me behind a dumpster. "Drugs, prostitution, you name it. Again, just a rumor."

"Who might know more?"

"Doug Lincoln, but you sent him to jail."

I could still pay the man a visit, although I doubted he would tell me anything. "Thanks, Mary. You're a big help as usual. Let me know if you hear anything else. Oh, have you happened to see Johnson with any police officers on a regular basis?"

"Yep. That Detective Warren."

Wow. Pay dirt. I hunted up Rod Looper next. He hadn't found a best friend since Ben Jones's death. I hoped he'd still be willing to talk to me.

I found him sweeping outside the makeup trailers. "How you doing, Rod?"

"Fair to middlin'. You?"

"I'm okay. Do you have a minute?"

"Another mystery?"

I grinned. "Of course. I'd like to know what you might know about William Johnson, Senior, needing protection for illegal activities."

"No beating around the bush for you, is there?" He motioned for me to have a seat in one of the lawn chairs outside a trailer. "He might own the studio, but he's not a good man."

"Drugs? Prostitution?"

Rod nodded. "So rumor says."

"You haven't seen it yourself?"

"Nope, and I've been working here as long as he's owned the place." He put a weathered hand on my arm. "Be careful asking questions about him. His son might have been murdered, not only because of the things he was doing, but because of what his father was involved in too."

I shuddered. "I will." I planted an impulsive kiss on his cheek. "Thank you."

"Anytime, girl." He stood and continued sweeping. "Try not to get yourself killed."

"I'll do my best." I still had almost an hour before returning to filming and opened the door to the trailer I shared with Ruthie. As I'd hoped, Lisa, our makeup artist, computer genius and hacker was inside.

She glanced up from putting away her supplies. "Need a touch-up?"

"No, I'd like to use your brain again. This has to be kept hush hush."

She clapped her hands. "My favorite way to use my brain. Who are we snooping on this time?"

"William Johnson, Senior."

Her eyes widened on her freckled face. "Really? What I am looking for?"

"A reason he would need to pay the police to keep his activities quiet."

"I'll get started right away."

"Thanks. I'll pay you for your time."

"Oh, no, you won't." Her eyes sparkled. "This is fun for me."

Knowing she'd dig as deep as she could and didn't need my help, I went in search of Brock and food. I found him alone in the cafeteria with a laptop opened in front of him. "This is unusual for you."

"Eating here or the laptop?" He smiled.

"Both."

"I'm digging through old files of newspapers in the hopes of finding something…anything."

I sat across from him and stole a fry from his tray. "I've got Lisa working on it."

"Good." He closed his laptop. "I stink at research. Let me get you something to eat."

"Salad and diet soda, please." I sat back and watched as every female head in the place swiveled to watch him move. Look all you want, ladies, the man is mine. The thought still sent a thrill through me.

Brock seemed oblivious to the attention and returned with a large salad. The warm look in his eyes said I was the only one in the room who mattered to him. How had I gotten so lucky?

While we ate, I recounted what I'd learned from Mary and Rod, being careful to leave out their names in case any Nosy Nelly's sat nearby. "We're close, Brock. I can feel it."

"The closer we get, the more danger you're in."

"*We're* in." I wiggled my eyebrows and tossed Shutterbug a carrot. She bit once and swallowed. Why did dogs crave treats so much but gobble them up too fast to taste them?

"Have you purchased a gun yet?"

"No, but I do have a Taser."

"Better than nothing, I guess." He leaned back in his chair. "I can't believe I'm with a woman who craves danger. I always thought I'd be with someone like my mother."

"Stay at home and look after the kids?"

His mouth crooked. "Something like that."

"Disappointed?"

He reached across the table and covered my hand. "Not in the least. You're way more fun."

A quick glance at the clock on the wall and I wolfed down my lunch. Standing, I placed a kiss on Brock's lips. "Gotta go. See you for dinner?"

"Wouldn't miss it. Go ahead. I'll take care of your tray."

I raced out the door and arrived on set with two minutes to spare. Louie took one look at my hair falling free of the ponytail Lisa had carefully sprayed into place and yelled, "Makeup!"

The lady on set wasn't nearly as gentle. By the time she'd finished tugging, I felt as if my hair was two inches longer. I took my place in front of an actor playing dead.

"Cut." Louie groaned. "Come on, Canyon. Act like you did when you found Georgia's body?"

I whirled to face him. How did he know I was the one who had found her?

Chapter Twelve

"How did you know about that?" I stepped off set and grabbed his arm, pulling him into a secluded corner.

He yanked free. "Everyone knows."

I narrowed my eyes. "How?"

"Ruthie's been talking about it all morning. Get a grip, Canyon." He marched back to the set and pointed. "Get to work."

Someone really needed to learn how to keep her lips closed. It wouldn't do for Ruthie to tell all when we were trying to lay a trap. I shot her a glare, then transformed into a startled cop who had just found her prime witness dead.

"What?" Ruthie asked on the way to our trailer. "Did I do something to make you mad? I thought you were going to hit the poor man hired as an extra."

"Yes, Grandma, I'm upset with you." I reached

for the door handle. "You can't be telling people everything that goes on while we're trying to solve these murders. You'll tip off the killer by doing so."

"Sorry. I get excited over the attention sometimes."

I rolled my eyes and let her climb the steps ahead of me.

Lisa sat hunched over her laptop, fingers flying over the keys. "Makeup remover towelettes on the counter. I'm in the middle of something."

Who was I to argue about someone not doing their job when they were doing me a favor. I pulled a towelette from the box and scrubbed at my stage makeup.

I started to say something, but Lisa put up a finger. "Shh."

Okay. I sat on the sofa and watched.

Her brows furrowed over her freckled nose. Her red hair had come loose from its ponytail. From the looks of her, Lisa had been hard at work for a while.

"What is she doing?" Ruthie whispered as she sat next to me.

"Trying to find dirt on William Johnson."

"Hmm." Ruthie thought for a moment. "You know how we found the drug house his son frequented? Well, the father frequents a different type of house."

"What do you mean?" I tilted my head.

"Ladies of the evening, or so rumor goes. Maybe he goes there not because he, uh, you know, but because he owns it?"

"Got an address!" Lisa grinned and turned up the music on her phone, then put a finger to her lips

"I found several houses and warehouses owned by Mr. Johnson," she whispered. "This one looks the most promising as a house of ill repute."

I took the piece of paper she waved at me. "Why this one?"

"It's right on the border between a nice neighborhood and a bad one."

I didn't understand her reasoning, but it was worth checking out. "You are the best, Lisa. Really, you should work for the police department," I whispered.

"Nah, I like being my own boss." She packed up her laptop and supplies. "See you two bright and early in the morning."

As Ruthie, the two dogs in tow, and I headed for my car, I asked, "Do you want to go check out the house?"

"Not without our men, I don't." She climbed into the passenger seat of my Volkswagen, keeping a tight grip on a squirming Sassy.

I opened the back door to let Shutterbug in. "I don't think it would be good for Brock's good-boy reputation to be seen there."

"Then we'll take Morgan."

"I'm not going to a whorehouse!" Morgan crossed his arms and shook his head, not bothering to reach for the door. "What if someone sees me?"

"Better you than Brock," I said. "We need to find out whether Johnson owns the place and knows what is going on."

"So, you want me to go in alone."

"Stop being such a baby," Ruthie told him, patting his arm. "I think a big strong fella like you can fend off women."

"I don't like it." He exhaled heavily. "I suppose you want to go now?"

Ruthie and I nodded in unison.

"Can we at least wait until dark?"

I shrugged. "If that makes you feel better."

When Brock arrived for dinner, he insisted on accompanying Morgan. "No one is going to say anything about seeing me there. I think the women will be so thrilled to see me that they'll tell me anything I want to know." He winked.

"Big ego." He might be right. While I didn't like the idea, a starstruck hooker might be our best bet at finding out information. "Fine, but Ruthie and I will be waiting right outside in the van we rented earlier this afternoon."

"That won't be conspicuous at all." Morgan frowned. "Done much staking out?"

I narrowed my eyes. "No, but no one will suspect a simple van like a soccer mom might drive."

"If you say so." Morgan glanced at Brock. "You seem to be looking forward to going."

"It'll be something new." His eyes twinkled.

"I want both of you to wear a wire," I said. Jealousy wasn't something I experienced much, but it welled up in me like a stopped-up sink. "This way, we can hear what's going on and catch something you'll miss."

Brock's grin let me know he knew exactly what I was up to and liked it. "Sure thing, babe. Where are we going to get wired?"

"I have that stuff in my room," Morgan said. "I

came prepared when Kelly asked me to watch over Ruthie. You never know what crazy scheme these two will come up with next."

Thirty minutes later the men were wired and the four of us with three dogs in the back drove to the address Lisa had found. We parked two houses down, in the good neighborhood, and stared at the unassuming, two-story, white-sided house. Extensions, obviously added after the house was built, made it the largest building in the whole area—good or bad.

"Looks like a strange layout," I said. "You men have your mics on?"

"Yep." Morgan shoved open the door. "Come on, movie star. Let's get this over with. Pray for us, ladies, as we enter a lion's den."

Brock bounded out with more joy than sour-faced Morgan. He rubbed his hands together. "Adventure waits."

I rolled my eyes and sighed. Did Brock just want me around because I kept his life interesting? Maybe he was one of those adrenaline junkies.

The two men strolled to the front door. The loud sound of knocking almost burst my eardrums. I reached up and turned down the volume on my earpiece.

"Yes?" A woman answered the door.

"Huh." Ruthie leaned closer to the windshield. "She's wearing classy slacks and a long-sleeved blouse."

"You didn't expect her to answer the door wearing lingerie, did you?"

"Yes, actually."

"Shh. I need to hear."

She huffed and bounced back against the seat. "So do I."

"Yeah, we, uh," Morgan stammered, "came for fun?"

"No fun here." She started to close the door.

"Johnson sent us."

The woman remained silent for a moment, then glanced up and down the street. "Hurry up before the neighbors get suspicious. Next time use the proper verbiage."

Uh-oh. They were almost busted before stepping foot inside.

"Wait. Aren't you Brock Hanson?" The woman asked.

"Yes, ma'am."

"Oh my, the girls will be fighting over you."

I wanted to gag.

"I'm just here to talk," Brock said. "Maybe someone new?"

Oh, my man was smart.

"I have just the girl. You, big man, will have my top girl."

"I want to slap her," Ruthie said.

"Let me show you to a room where you will be joined by your evening companion." The sound of heels clicking against a wood floor followed. Then a door opened, then another. "Just a minute."

"I'm in," Brock said.

"Me, too," Morgan said.

"The two of you behave." I upped the volume on my earpiece.

"Wouldn't think of doing anything else." Brock

laughed. His laugh was cut short as the door opened.

"Oh…my…gosh," a young voice gushed. "It really is you."

"In the flesh."

"And you only want to talk?" Her voice clearly said she had other things on her mind.

"Yes. As a celebrity, I'm surrounded by people, but I rarely have anyone I can talk to."

Did I mention my man was good?

"I'm cutting off Morgan's mic on my piece," I told Ruthie. "You listen to him. It's too much going on inside my head otherwise."

Ruthie nodded. Her brows furrowed. "His girl is a skank. She keeps coming on to him."

Really? What did my grandmother expect?

"How does a young girl like you get mixed up in something like this?" Brock asked.

"I want to be a star. Can you help me?"

"You think this job is a step in the right direction?"

"Someone told me it was. I get to meet a lot of big names in the industry."

"Name one."

"I can't. It's not allowed."

"I'll introduce you to my agent if you do."

Oh, Brock. Resorting to bribery.

Ruthie slapped the dashboard. "Keep turning her down, Morgan, or you won't know what hit you."

I grinned and kept my focus on Brock. Come on, girl. Give us a name.

"All right." Her voice lowered. "You can't tell a

soul. Promise me you'll introduce me to your agent."

"I promise."

"The man who told me this would help me become a star was William Johnson. He owns this place."

Chapter Thirteen

Brock started talking the moment they entered the van. "That paid off," Brock said, a huge grin on his face. "It looks like a regular house on the inside. Maybe a few risqué paintings on the walls, but pretty normal."

"I don't care what the inside looks like," I said, rounding the corner.

"I do." Ruthie patted Brock's arm. "Is it all red and velvety?"

"What?" He frowned. "No, normal like I said. The room I was in had a blue and white quilt on the bed and white curtains on the window."

"Let's talk about the bombshell." I glanced in the rearview mirror at Morgan. "What did you find out, Morgan?"

"That I never want to go in a place like that again. My girl didn't want to talk. It was like fighting off an octopus."

"You poor thing." Ruthie chuckled. "It must have been a horrible experience."

"It was!"

"Well, we got what we came for." I headed down the freeway. "Now to prove that Johnson owns the house. It shouldn't be too hard."

"Even if his name is on the deed, he could say he rents it out and doesn't know what goes on inside," Brock pointed out. "You'll have to get photos or raid the place while he's there."

Not so easy after all. I sighed. "Maybe Lori could stake the place out."

Brock leaned over and whispered in my ear, "Why don't you and I do it? It might be fun, we'd be alone…"

Goosebumps broke out on my skin. I bit my bottom lip and nodded, pretty sure that if we were alone in a dark car for hours on end, we wouldn't be paying attention to what went on in the house. I cleared my throat. "Okay."

"Not without me, you don't," Morgan said. "I'm here to protect you, remember? Which means if you go, we all go."

My shoulders slumped. Talk about a killjoy. "We'll go tomorrow night and every night thereafter until we catch him."

"Every night?" Ruthie groaned. "We'll be exhausted filming each day. I need my beauty sleep, Kelly."

"Then we'll ask Lori." I did want to go. Maybe Morgan would loosen the leash if I went with his sister.

The next morning, I sat in the makeup chair

while Lisa readied me for the day's filming. Knowing either Ruthie or I would say something, Morgan had checked the trailer for bugs. Thankfully, the place was clean and we were free to speak.

"I can't believe the fun you guys have," Lisa said, unpinning my hair from the top of my head. "I mean, I enjoy digging on the web, but to actually go and do stuff…that sounds like a blast."

"It's dangerous." I winced as she teased my hair to look as if I'd been in a fight.

"I don't mind danger."

I swiveled in my chair. "You're serious?"

She nodded. "I want to do more to help you find those killers and write your books."

"Let me think about it, okay?" I turned back around. There were already more people nosing around than was safe. I'd prefer Lisa stay danger-free behind her computer screen, but I wasn't her boss and couldn't stop her if she set out to ask questions on her own.

"Oh." Ruthie stood in the doorway looking outside. "You'll never guess who just showed up on the lot."

"No time for guessing. Who?" I stood to let Ruthie take my place in the chair.

"William Johnson, Senior."

"Really?" I rushed to the door. The owner of the studio strolled among the trailers as if he didn't have a care in the world. Two steps behind him trailed a muscle-packing Black man. Bodyguard, perhaps? What had happened to make him think he needed one?

I shoved open the door and grabbed my camera bag. "Stay, Shutterbug. Ruthie, I'll meet you on set." I darted down the steps and followed the two men at what I hoped was a safe distance. Of course, if they noticed me, I did belong. I hung my camera around my neck.

The two men stopped outside the cafeteria. I ducked behind a dumpster and snapped a photo.

"Why do you think Brock Hanson felt the need to visit Maggie's place?" Johnson stared up into the other man's face. "He can have any woman he wants. Not to mention he's in a relationship with that nosy Canyon dame."

"Some men are married and still visit cathouses," his companion shrugged. "Doesn't mean anything."

"Hmm." Johnson glanced around them. "If they find out I own the place and pay off the cops with the proceeds to look the other way, all will be for nothing." He poked the big man in the chest. "I hired you to make sure that doesn't happen, Harrelson."

I really wished I had a tape recorder with me. Again, I had confirmation of a dirty cop and no proof other than hearsay.

"What do you want me to do?" Harrelson crossed his large arms. "Protect you? Take care of threats? You'll have to be more specific."

"Keep Canyon and her nosy grandmother out of my hair." Johnson yanked open the cafeteria door and stepped inside.

I plastered my back against the block wall behind the dumpster. The hunter had become the hunted. Now with a hired giant paid to keep me in line, I didn't want to end up like my father. But if I died after identifying his murderer, my death wouldn't be in vain.

A quick glance at my watch sent me dashing for the set where my furry best friend met me at the door. Louie glared from under lowered brows and shot a glimpse at the clock on the wall.

"Two minutes to spare," I said, grinning.

"Too close for comfort. Makeup! Get rid of the sheen on her forehead." Louie stomped to his director's chair. "Let's get to work."

By lunchtime, we'd wrapped up the day's filming, and Louie told us we could go home and he'd see us in the morning.

On the way to my car, I dialed Lori's number. "What time are you picking me up tonight?"

"Nine."

"I've got more confirmation that Johnson owns that house." I told her about the conversation between him and Harrelson. I almost told her about the threat made against me, but kept my mouth shut. If word got out, it would be three-to-one keeping me behind lock and key. "See you later." I clicked off my phone and slid into the driver's seat to wait on Ruthie.

Fifteen minutes later, she approached at a fast pace. "Sorry." She set Sassy in the back seat. "I got a call that the Thunderbird is ready to be picked up." She clicked her seat belt into place. "I don't want to take that car anywhere until this case is solved. Can't risk the damage." She cut me a sharp glance. "So, I bought the rental van."

"You want me to drive the van everywhere?" I shuddered.

"Yes. I don't care if it gets destroyed. It's an ugly beast."

Painted the color of pea-green soup, the van couldn't be uglier. Not to mention it was shaped like a toaster. A pea-green toaster. I almost hoped someone would blow it up. Not while anyone was in it, of course. Well, maybe it wouldn't be such a bad thing if the person responsible for Dad's death happened to be inside.

"What's so funny?" Ruthie asked.

"Nothing. Just daydreaming about justice."

She reached over and touched my arm. "We'll find the person who killed Kevin. Maybe not today or this week, but we will find them. I know it in here." She moved her hand to her heart.

"Thank you, Grandma." I smiled, blinking away the tears.

"Absolutely not." Brock shook his head, his features appearing as hard as carved stone. "You are not going on a stakeout without me."

"I'm going with Lori." I cupped his cheek. "I couldn't be safer. Right, Morgan?"

"I think Brock should go with the two of you."

Brock grinned. "You're outnumbered."

"Fine." I turned and looked in my camera bag, which was quickly turning into my crime-solving bag. I had my camera, Taser, pepper spray, flashlight, and my notebook. Everything a nosy photographer needed.

The doorbell rang. Morgan peered through the peephole, then opened the door to let Lori in. She took one look at Brock's face.

"Fine. Let's get this show on the road. Movie stars sit in the back." She spun around and marched to her dark green sedan and opened the door. "With the dog."

Shutterbug bounded past us and into the seat. She gave one bark and waited, clearly excited to go on another adventure.

I gripped Brock's hand and squeezed. "It's not so bad having you along." I winked and slid into the passenger seat.

"Come on, handsome." Lori laughed. "Just sit in the back and look pretty."

"I can provide the muscle if needed." He climbed in and slammed the door. "I'm not just a pretty face."

Lori glanced at me and laughed. "Let's go catch a naughty man."

Chapter Fourteen

We parked outside Melanie's place for the third night in a row, coffee in hand. Late nights and early mornings at the set had me feeling like a zombie. I stared through the rearview mirror at Brock who had pulled a pair of binoculars from somewhere.

"What?" Brock asked, not lowering the binoculars. "This is all research for my acting…and your books."

Lori laughed. "You're a trip, Hanson. Now hunker down in your seat and stay out of sight."

"Have you heard anything that's happening at the precinct?" I asked, unbuckling my seatbelt and slouching as ordered.

"No one tells me anything. Not even that new rookie, although I think he's clean." She shrugged. "He's heard things about me, I'm sure, so why trust me?"

"Maybe I could talk to him?"

"It would only get back to Warren. We really need to find his connection in all this. Something irrefutable." She straightened. "There's Johnson."

The man didn't knock on the front door. Instead, he waltzed in as an owner would. I snapped a couple of pictures. "Brock, get your cell phone and go inside. Catch him in the act. Proof of entry might not be enough to prove he's doing anything wrong."

"I've got someone looking up the deed," Lori said. "But catching him in the act would be better."

"I'm not sure they'd buy the 'I only want to talk' trick again." Brock lowered the binoculars.

"Sure, they would. You're just a lonely celebrity looking for an unbiased person to have a conversation with." I shifted in my seat to grin at him.

"Not really. That girl wants me to hook her up with my agent and I haven't done that yet."

I yawned. "I'll take Shutterbug for a walk and see if I can find out anything. Hand me that baseball cap behind the seat."

"Stay within sight," Lori ordered.

"You're letting her go out there?" Brock leaned on the front seat and handed me the cap. "What if someone is hiding in the shadows?"

"Waiting to jump out and grab me?" I tugged the hat onto my head. "In this neighborhood? I promise not to stray too far into the rough side." I got out, opened the back door for Shutterbug to jump down, then clipped her leash to her collar. "My Taser is in my pocket. I'm good."

First, I strolled past the house as if it were

nothing new and stopped a few yards past the next one. The houses further down the street sported overgrown lawns and hoodlums in wife beaters. A few wolf whistles came my way. I ignored them and slipped between Melanie's place and her neighbor's. As long as Shutterbug didn't seem worried, I figured we were safe.

A back gate to the neighbor's house swung open at my touch. Surprising, considering their proximity to the lower income houses.

A concrete block fence lured me as a prime spot to perch and try to catch a glimpse of Johnson through a window. Leaving Shutterbug to guard from the ground, I scuttled up the fence and straddled it.

The curtains were open in the kitchen. I focused my camera lens and waited, praying no one spotted me sitting up there like a target in navy blue.

Wait a minute. Johnson stepped into the kitchen with the same woman who had answered the door during our last visit. She handed him a thick envelope. I continued to snap pictures as he removed and counted out a large amount of cash.

Shutterbug barked.

Johnson spun toward the window.

I jerked and fell despite my flailing arms, landing with a hard thud on my back in the neighbor's yard. Once I caught my breath, I dashed through the gate and across the street, resuming what I hoped looked like nothing more than a woman walking her dog.

Until I spotted Harrelson climbing out of Johnson's black Mercedes. He glanced my way and

I stooped to tie my shoe, peering up from under the brim of my cap.

Shutterbug barked.

Harrelson narrowed his eyes.

Darn. I'd forgotten how unforgettable my dog was. Had the man seen her before? I didn't think so. My breathing returned to normal when he entered the house.

I darted for the van and threw myself headfirst into the driver's seat as Brock held the back door open for my dog. "Time to go." I turned the key in the ignition and peeled rubber down the street.

"What did you find?" Lori asked.

"Why is there dirt on the back of your shirt?" Brock asked.

"I'll explain it all in a minute." My heartrate threatened to rise into emergency-room levels. I gripped the steering wheel with sweaty palms and veered into the vacant parking lot of a drugstore.

Heart still racing, I turned. "I got pictures of Melanie handing Johnson a lot of cash."

"Great!" Lori grinned. "That could be the proof we need. Now to find the cop he's paying off."

"How?"

"I don't know." Her smile faded. "With me off the case and suspended, it'll be more of a challenge. You wouldn't want to flirt with the rookie, would you?" Her lips twitched.

"No, I did that once with Louie with disastrous results." I shuddered. Thankfully, he'd caught on to my deceit and ordered me out of his office.

She glanced at Brock. "Too bad there aren't any female cops. Wait a minute. You set that gal up with your agent, then be real sweet to her. Maybe she knows who the cop is."

"I'm not going to toy with her affections." Brock crossed his arms. "That wouldn't be nice." His eyes widened.

I glanced out the window. Six African American young men surrounded the van. One tapped on the window with a knife.

"Show them your badge," I told Lori.

"Not on your life. They kill cops around here."

They looked like they had malice in their hearts for all three of us. I rolled my window down an inch. "Can we help you?"

"Yeah. What's three white people doing in our hood? And why were you snooping around old woman Jones's house?"

"Uh, my dog ran off."

"Lady, we watched you the whole time. You were up to no good." The shortest, stockiest of the group stepped forward. Ah.

"Hello, Jerard."

He grinned. "We're messin' with you. But seriously, what brings you over here?"

His grin reminded me of a shark ready to take a bite out of his prey. "Working surveillance for research on a book. Practice, you know?" I put on my most convincing face. I don't think he bought my answer.

"Enough of this." Brock leaned over the seat. "What do you guys know about the whorehouse?"

Jerard clammed up as if someone tried to steal his pearl. He sent the other guys a look that told them to keep their mouths shut.

"What's the name of the cop being paid to keep his mouth shut?" I lowered my window another inch and snapped my fingers to stop Shutterbug's barking.

Jerard made the motion of locking his lips and throwing away the key. He stepped back, the others following. Seconds later, they disappeared into the shadows.

"That dude looked scared," Lori said.

"As if he thought he was being watched." I glanced back in the direction we'd come just in time to see a black Mercedes round the corner. "Jerard knows. He lied when we caught him in the beach house. He knows exactly who hired him to shut me up." I wish I knew what they thought I knew.

"Let's go home. I'm filming an action scene tomorrow, and I ache from falling off the fence," I said, yawning.

"You fell off the fence?" Brock flowered.

"It was the perfect place to take pictures from. I fell when Johnson turned around. I didn't want him to see me."

"What if he did?"

"Then he has confirmation that we suspect him." Which upped the danger level. I left out Harrelson watching me when I headed back to the van. No reason to worry Brock any more than he was. Right?

Sure. Keep it close to the chest until I had to tell the others. Maybe that would keep most of the danger focused on me.

Chapter Fifteen

"I need you to look into a young man named Jerard something. He's a gang member, I think," I said the instant I entered our trailer the next morning. "He's the one who tried to assault me at the beach house."

"That should be easy." Lisa held out a vinyl apron, fastening it around my neck after I sat in the chair. "Anything in particular I'm looking for?"

"Any connection to William Johnson or some big dude named Harrelson who acts as Johnson's bodyguard."

"Got it. I'll work on it as soon as you and Ruthie leave." She loosened my hair from its ponytail. "I don't think I'll ever understand why I have to make your hair look like you've been running around, when running around will give it the same look."

I shrugged. "I don't do all my stunts. Maybe that's why."

"Oh, a note was left here for you this morning. I found it on the table." She handed me a plain white envelope.

I opened it. "Johnson wants to hire me for a photo shoot."

"With a gun most likely," Ruthie said from her place on the sofa. She peered from under her sleep mask. "Take Morgan with you. Oh, I guess that means we all go." She let the mask fall back into place. Every morning she insisted I have my makeup done first so she could snatch a little more beauty sleep.

"I agree with Ruthie." Lisa pulled up a handful of my hair and started back combing. "It's a trap."

I agreed, but that idiot side of me that trod where danger resided whispered in my ear that it might be a good opportunity to do some digging. "It can't be too bad if the whole gang is there."

"You're either brave or stupid," Lisa said.

"Go with the second." I laughed.

When Lisa finished with me and was working on Ruthie, I took the time to read over the day's script. I would be shot. Something I needed to work on. Falling on purpose wasn't exactly a talent of mine. I looked awkward, fake, and ended up with bruises. A long day loomed ahead of me.

By nine a.m., late as usual, Ruthie, Shutterbug, and I arrived on set. Louie muttered something under his breath about taking an early retirement and fell back into his chair. "I'm buying you a watch."

"No need," Ruthie said. "My fault this time. I couldn't get going this morning."

"Late night?" He scowled.

"Yes." She glanced at me. Ruthie had refused to go to sleep until I returned home safe.

"Some people do not take their careers serious enough. Places, everyone."

Ruthie and I hunkered behind a pile of wooden crates. The lights dimmed. The set had been transformed to look like an alley between two tall brick buildings. Set designers didn't get the credit they deserved. Yesterday, this set was a police department.

Blanks were fired back and forth between us and the 'bad' guys. I rose slightly and motioned for Ruthie to head to the dumpster. A shot rang out from above us.

I whirled and dropped like a sack of potatoes. No acting required. Someone had really shot me, and it hurt.

"Kelly!" Ruthie leaned over me as the other actors and Louie darted over.

"Ow." I pressed to a sitting position. "I thought we were using blanks, not real ones." I snatched a rubber bullet from the floor.

"I, uh…" the actor who had shot me dropped his gun. "I checked it before…I left to go to the bathroom."

"Who had access to these weapons?" Louie glared at everyone. "Well?"

Relieved to be alive, but achy, I struggled to my feet. The warning convinced me more than ever that the solution to this mystery hovered in front of me. I just had to see it. I put a hand to my ribcage and lowered myself onto one of the crates. "Give me a minute. I'll be fine."

"Call the police and check those guns again," Louie ordered before favoring me with a grin "We filmed the fall. Most realistic fall you've ever done."

"Ha ha."

By the time Detective Warren and Officer Banks arrived, I'd regained my breath. To my relief, Banks approached to take my statement.

"You drew the short straw, huh?" I said.

"What?" He blinked.

"Never mind. I know the drill. Someone shot me with a rubber bullet. They don't want me dead…yet, or they would have used a real one. I have no idea who shot me. Well, yeah, the actor did, but I don't know who put the bullet in the gun."

"Someone wants you dead?"

I stared up at him. Could it be possible Warren hadn't mentioned what I was up to? "May I talk to you in private, Officer?"

"Why?"

I got up and walked away, hoping he'd follow. He did. I smiled. Curiosity always won. Out of sight of the set, I pivoted toward him. "How much has Warren told you about me? Anything about his former partner, Lawrence?"

"Ma'am, I'm the one asking the questions." High spots of color appeared on his cheeks.

"Throw me a bone, Officer. I can be quite annoying."

He grabbed my arm and pulled me further into the shadows. "Miss Canyon, asking questions gets people into trouble. Surely, Detective Lawrence has explained that to you."

"So, you do know something!"

"Hush before you get us both killed." He slipped me a business card. "Have Detective Lawrence call me." With that, he whirled around and marched away, leaving me staring at his cell phone number. Awesome. I slipped the card into my pocket and rejoined the others. We very possibly had found our dirty cop at the precinct.

Once the police had taken everyone's statement and checked the weapons for real, or rubber, bullets, we resumed filming. Louie couldn't stop saying how they should always use rubber bullets because of the realism. I wanted to punch him.

From the stormy expression on Brock's face later that evening, he wanted to strangle me. "Someone shot you?"

"Someone shot you?" Lori asked, entering the living room.

"With a rubber bullet. I'm fine." I plopped onto the sofa and grinned. "But, when I tried to question Officer Banks, he gave me his card and said for you to call him."

"Really?" Lori's eyebrows rose.

"Don't change the subject, Kelly." Brock's face paled. "You aren't even safe on the set."

"Sure I am. If someone wanted me dead, they'd have substituted the blank with a real bullet." I held out my hand.

After a moment's hesitation, he took it and sat

next to me. He leaned his forehead against mine. "You scare me."

"Sometimes I scare myself."

"Wait until you hear that she's doing a photo shoot at Johnson's house." Ruthie set a tray of coffee mugs on the table.

"What?" Morgan frowned over Sassy's head.

"Exactly what she said. I know. You'll go with me. Thus, I'll be perfectly safe." I gave Brock a quick kiss and reached for a mug.

"You crave danger." Brock grabbed a mug and held it out for Ruthie to fill.

"Not really. I crave justice."

"Sometimes that's the same thing." He looked so worried my heart lurched.

"I'll be fine."

"Your father wasn't fine."

Ouch. I blew into my mug.

"I'll be right back." Lori ducked into the dining room. She returned a few minutes later to let us know that Officer Banks would be here in twenty minutes.

"Can we trust him?" Morgan asked.

"We're about to find out," she said. "Kelly, see if Lisa can do an in-depth, real fast, check on our alleged rookie."

I sent Lisa a quick text. Seconds later she replied yes. "So, you think he's undercover?"

Lori's eyebrows raised. "Sometimes your quick mind astounds me. Yes, I suspect he is."

"If Lisa can check on him, then our killer could to," I said.

"Not if they don't suspect. I believe he's one of

the good ones."

Made sense. Half way through our twenty-minute wait, Lisa called. "He's a cop, originally from San Francisco. He volunteered for the job here upon Lawrence's suspension. Anything else?"

"That's it, thanks. Unless you want to dig more."

"Oh, I do." Click.

By the time Banks arrived, my anticipation reared up like ocean waves, ebbing and flowing until I couldn't sit still. When the doorbell rang, I leaped to my feet, only to be stopped by Morgan holding up his hand.

"You know the drill, Canyon."

I sighed and plopped back down.

Banks, dressed in jeans and a button-down maroon shirt stepped into the room. "Is this place secure?"

"Yes, I checked it myself." Morgan motioned to an empty armchair.

"Why are you here?" Lori asked. "Why did you ask for the reassignment?"

Banks glanced at me. "Because two years ago I did a DNA test and found out Detective Kevin Canyon is my biological father."

I dropped my mug, spilling coffee all over Ruthie's oriental rug. I had a brother? "Who is your mother?"

"Rhonda Banks. Deceased. Former schoolteacher."

"My fourth-grade teacher?" Blood drained from my face to my feet.

Ruthie sighed. "He dated her before Lori, soon

after your mother's death, Kelly. Welcome to this crazy family, Officer Banks. You must be close to Kelly's age. Kevin turned to Rhonda out of grief, the summer before Kelly started the fifth grade."

"Ma'am. I hate to tell you this, but my father dated my mother while married to Mrs. Canyon."

"Dad had an affair?" Not possible. "Grandma?"

"Your parents separated for a while," she waved a dismissive hand. "He wouldn't have really cheated. Your mother had a hard time dealing with his hours as a street cop. She got pregnant with you right after their reconciliation."

The room sat in stunned silence for a few minutes before Lori cleared her throat. "I hate to break up this family reunion, and you might possibly be Kevin's son, but that's not the real reason you're here. Is it?"

Banks shook his head. "When I discovered who my father was, I read about his death. I did some digging and thought everything looked fishy. So, here I am to confirm whether my instincts are correct." He pulled a sheet of paper from his jean's pocket. "Here is the proof of my identity. I'm here to help you find my father's killer."

"You're in the best position." Lori glanced at the paper. "Someone in the precinct is dirty and taking protection money from William Johnson. We need proof of who the dirty cop is."

Chapter Sixteen

I woke the next morning gritty-eyed from lack of sleep over trying to figure out how to find proof on Johnson and his cop buddy. Warren was dirty, but I had nothing more to go on other than a gut feeling.

Hopefully, I'd have time to snoop a little at the photo shoot to get dirt on Johnson, and my newly-discovered half-brother could find out something on Warren. I didn't think I'd ever get used to having Banks as a brother. He did have Dad's eyes and square jaw.

Swinging my legs over the side of the bed, I sat up and groaned. Five a.m. on a Saturday. Ugh.

Now to convince everyone I didn't need an entourage at the Johnsons'. Ruthie and Morgan would be the most difficult. Morgan wouldn't want to leave Ruthie behind, even with Brock watching her, and I couldn't snoop effectively with my loose-lipped grandmother trotting behind me.

I entered the kitchen and dropped into a chair across from Morgan. "Just you today. Ruthie talks too much."

"Absolutely not." He shook his head while shoveling a forkful of pancakes into his mouth. "We all go or no one goes."

"Brock can stay with her. I can leave Shutterbug too, if you want." I straightened in my chair. "Come on. You know I can snoop better without worrying about what's going to come out of her mouth."

He pointed his fork at me. "No."

Ugh. I felt like a scolded child.

Ruthie set a plate of pancakes in front of me. "I'll keep my mouth shut, sweetie."

"Nothing personal."

"No offense taken." She patted my shoulder before taking her seat. "I'm thinking of hiring a chef."

"That's a random comment." I buttered my breakfast and sprinkled powdered sugar across the top.

"I've been thinking about it for a while. I'm tired of cooking, and eating out all the time isn't healthy. I'll start interviewing tomorrow."

Morgan, the joy killer, shook his head. "Not until this case is resolved. Posing as a chef would be an easy way to get to you."

"I'd get references." Ruthie frowned. "I'm not an imbecile."

I grinned and forked a bite into my mouth. I'd like to see how Ruthie finagled Morgan into getting her way.

"Do you know what confuses me?" he said.

"No, honey. What?"

"Why two smart women are so stupid as to willingly put themselves in danger." He started to fork another bite of food, but Ruthie whipped his plate out from under him faster than a snake lashed at a passing leg.

"Well, if I'm that stupid, you can find someone else to cook your meals." She marched to the kitchen with his plate.

Morgan shrugged and slid her plate in front of him. "More than one way to get food."

"You'd better be fast. She won't be gone—"

Ruthie snatched the second plate and ate standing up, glaring at Morgan all the while.

"I said you were smart."

"You said we were stupid after that, which cancels out the first thing you said."

"Are you two having your first fight?" I grinned and finished my breakfast before Morgan thought of stealing it too.

Ruthie smiled. "We fight all the time. That keeps the fire in our relationship."

Morgan laughed. "Your grandmother is a firecracker. Red, hot…"

"Okay. Enough. Gross." I picked up my empty plate. "How will I explain the two of you to Johnson?"

"Easy." Ruthie's grin widened, yet her gaze never left Morgan. "This dear man is my bodyguard, Lots of celebrities have them, and I'm your assistant."

"No one will buy that you're my assistant."

"Fine. Simply say I was bored."

I shrugged. That might work. Anyone who knows Ruthie knows she doesn't always make a lot of sense. I set my plate in the kitchen sink and grabbed another pancake from the pan. Once it cooled, I tossed it to Shutterbug who caught it in midair.

"As much as I like the thrill of finding justice, I kind of miss the simple days of being a paparazzi." I patted her head. "Acting is hard. I'd rather write the books and take the pictures. Maybe I won't renew my contract. What do you say?"

Shutterbug's ears twitched.

"Great idea. I'll think and pray about it. I can't do anything for a few months anyway."

"Your contract is for the duration of the series, dear. What if it goes on for seven years as some shows do?" Ruthie set her plate next to mine. "Didn't you read before you signed?"

I sighed. "Not really. I skimmed."

"Don't fret. You're really good. Maybe you'll win an Emmy."

"Really?" That brightened me up. An award would be nice and make the work worth the effort.

Ruthie stared. "A lot of little girls dream of being an actress. The job falls into your lap and you aren't even appreciative."

"I'm trying to be." I grinned.

"You're hopeless. Keep taking your pictures as a hobby and concentrate on what's important."

"Acting is important?"

"Yes. It provides needed entertainment to people."

I hugged her. "Let's get ready to find our bad cop."

An hour later, three adults and two dogs were stuffed into the ugly-colored van heading toward Beverly Hills. We stopped at a ten-foot iron fence and I pressed the button on the intercom. "Kelly Canyon. Mr. Johnson is expecting me."

The gate swung open. I drove up a winding brick driveway and parked in front of a monstrous salmon-colored stucco mansion.

"Huh." Ruthie peered out the window. "I never would have guessed that the studio owner lived in a pink house."

"It doesn't matter." I pushed my door open. "We're here to find something useful in catching Dad's killer, not critique the man's decorating sense."

"Why can't we do both?" With Sassy in her arms, she climbed from the van.

With Morgan leading the way, as if someone were going to aim a gun out the window and shoot us right there in Richville, we approached the large double doors. Morgan rapped three times, then stepped back, his hand hovering at the small of his back where he'd stashed his weapon under his shirt.

A middle-aged woman in navy slacks and a white blouse answered the door. Her eyes widened at the sight of the dogs. "No dogs allowed in the house. You have to leave them here."

Ruthie started to say something, but kept her mouth shut and clipped a leash on Sassy.

I took the leash and hooked it to Shutterbug's collar. "Stay." She would, too, thus keeping Sassy from running off.

"I'm Ms. Davis, Mr. Johnson's housekeeper. You may come in and wait in the front room. He'll be with you shortly."

The front room was actually a great room, the size of half Ruthie's house. The place was as massive as a cathedral. Harrelson stood near a long wall of windows. His gaze flicked to us, but he remained as still as a statue. Morgan stood behind Ruthie and adopted the other man's stance.

"Good morning, lovely Canyon ladies." Johnson's gaze flicked over my jeans and tee-shirt. "Comfortable." He shook my hand, then turned to Ruthie, ignoring Morgan. "My dear." He airbrushed her cheek. "I'm glad to see that you are back in front of the camera where you belong."

"It's nice to be back." She gave a slight smile.

"Shall we get started?" I hitched my camera bag onto my shoulder.

"Yes, I'd like to take a couple of photos of just myself in my study, then a few of my wife and me in the backyard. Ah, there she is." He turned as a tall, thin, pretty woman in her thirties came down the hall.

Considering she looked close to the deceased Junior Johnson's age, I surmised she was not the first Mrs. Johnson. I held out my hand. "Nice to meet you."

"The same. Shall we?" She waved an arm toward the wall of windows.

Harrelson opened one that happened to be a door. His gaze landed on Morgan and hardened.

Uh-oh. Too much testosterone in the room. I

prayed it wouldn't come to a showdown between the two. Harrelson had to be twenty years younger than Morgan.

I followed Mrs. Johnson outside, Ruthie and Mr. Johnson following Morgan. Wow. An Olympic-size pool took precedence, but professional landscaping treated the eyes. Palm trees, flowers, and bushes trimmed in the shape of animals provided a relaxing area to spend a lazy afternoon.

"We thought the gazebo might be a good place," Mrs. Johnson said. "Natural light and flowers to add a touch of color. I've lunch prepared for after the photo session. I do hope you can stay."

"Perfect." Lunch might provide the perfect time to snoop. The house was large enough to get lost in. "You look familiar. Did you do any acting?"

She smiled. "A sitcom on the Disney channel when I was younger."

"That's right. *High School Mysteries*. You're Abbie Dunes. Loved that show." I set up my tripod. "Mr. Johnson, if you could join your wife."

Her smile faltered as his arm slipped around her waist. Only an observant person would notice how uncomfortable she seemed around her husband. Did she possibly know what kind of a man he was?

"I'm surprised that Brock Hanson isn't with you," Mr. Johnson said. "According to the tabloids, the two of you are inseparable."

"You shouldn't believe everything you read in the tabloids, sir." I positioned my camera. "Brock is out of town today filming." But, of course, the man knew that. He was baiting me for some reason.

I focused the camera. "Smile naturally." I

snapped away, taking photos from different angles and poses. Some of the couple sitting, some standing. Mrs. Johnson was right. The gazebo couldn't be more perfect as a backdrop. "Shall we move to the study, Mr. Johnson?"

"Yes. Ruthie can stay and keep my Abbie company." Not a request but an order.

Morgan looked torn. He didn't seem to know whether to go with me or stay with Ruthie.

"Go with Kelly," Ruthie said. "I'm perfectly fine with Abbie. We're going to talk films. You'll be bored." She waved a hand, playing up the part of him being her bodyguard.

He gave a curt nod and followed Mr. Johnson and me. From his taut jaw, it appeared as if Mr. Johnson was gritting his teeth. Oh, the man had something to say to me. I bit back a grin. Did he know I was on to him?

My smile faded. The green van. The very one parked outside his house had been at Melanie's place. How could we have missed that?

I grabbed Morgan's arm. "Excuse us a moment, Mr. Johnson. I need to talk to Mr. Morgan. I'll join you in just a moment." I pulled Morgan into a sitting room and closed the door. "He knows."

"Not possible."

"That stupid van. We drove it to Melanie's place. No one can mistake that horrible color."

He paled. "He won't try anything in his own home. You're safe enough today."

"Yeah, but what about tomorrow?"

Chapter Seventeen

"**Now then.**" I entered the study. "Where would you like your picture taken?"

"I thought perhaps behind my desk." His features were hard. "They're publicity shots."

"My specialty."

"That's right. You were paparazzi once." His eyes glittered. "I'm sure you know all kinds of secrets."

I locked gazes with him. "A few."

Morgan cleared his throat, warning me to tread carefully. I shot him a look and nodded. Contrary to popular belief, I knew what I was doing.

"I've wondered why Ruthie and you feel the need for a bodyguard."

"Why, do you have one?"

"I'm an influential man." Johnson rubbed his chin, his gaze piercing. "Who would want to harm two women?"

"We all have enemies, Mr. Johnson. Some appear as friendly as puppies, then go for the neck. Smile." I snapped a quick succession of photos, certain I caught a few of his hard expression before his public mask dropped into place.

The phone on his desk, a -gold-plated one reminiscent of the twenties, rang. I continued to take photos as he spoke to someone on the other end. Each time he glanced down, I'd snap a picture of a different section of the room.

He'd no sooner hung up than Mrs. Johnson announced lunch was served. "Are we finished here?" he asked.

I nodded. "I'll have the photos to you by sometime Monday. Then you may use them as you wish." After I thoroughly studied every single one. Of course, I'd leave out those I took without him.

"Let's eat." He rubbed his hands together. "We have a marvelous chef. One of the best, although I believe lunch will be a simple affair."

"Perhaps he could recommend someone to Ruthie." I packed up my equipment, conveniently dropping the lens cap.

"As long as she doesn't try to take mine." He grinned and motioned for me to exit before him. With one look behind us, he closed the door.

Lunch was served on the patio. Multiple choices of fancy sandwiches, an artfully designed fruit tray, pastries, and several flavors of tea. Simple and elegant. Ruthie had to be in her element. She loved fancy. Me…food was food.

"I've had some of the lunch meat served to your pets on the front porch," Mrs. Johnson said, taking her seat. "The little one is quite the rascal. It took Ruthie and me a bit of time to chase her down when the larger dog let go of the leash to eat."

"Rascal is a nice word for her," I said, filling my plate.

"Yes, but she's adorable. We secured her leash to the post." Mrs. Johnson smiled and served a plate full of food to her husband. "How was the shoot, dear?"

"Very good." He patted her arm. "We should consider a shoot for you."

She shrugged. "I have no need for publicity photos."

"Maybe you should get back into acting," Ruthie said. "You still have the looks. It's a great way to fill your time if you're bored."

"Abbie is anything but bored." Mr. Johnson speared Ruthie with a harsh glare. "She tends to my house and several charities. My wife is quite busy, aren't you, Abbie?"

"Quite." Her calm face gave little away, but something flickered in her eyes that told me she wouldn't be opposed to returning to acting.

Two-thirds of the way through my meal, I excused myself to go the restroom. Once I entered the house, I headed for the study bypassing several closed doors that might or might not be a bathroom. I'd have an easy excuse if I got caught.

I opened the study door and stepped inside, closing it behind me. I'd need a second of warning if someone came in. I pocketed the lens cap I'd dropped and hurried to the opposite side of the desk and studied the bookshelves.

Several ornate wooden boxes lay strategically placed as bookends and visual pleasures. I opened one and peered inside. Old coins. Another held vintage keys. Quite the collector, Mr. Johnson.

"What are you doing?"

I shrieked and whirled. I hadn't heard Morgan come in. "Stand guard outside the door and whistle if anyone comes."

"Like that isn't cliché."

"I dropped my lens cap and came to retrieve it."

"And snoop."

I smiled. "You know I can't let an opportunity go by." I waved my hand. "Go."

Too late. Abbie entered behind Morgan. "You shouldn't be in here."

I showed her the lens cap. "Just leaving."

"What you're looking for is in the file cabinet of his studio office. He isn't stupid enough to leave it here where I can find it."

My mouth opened and closed a few times. "You know what he does?"

"I'm not stupid either." She motioned her head toward the door. "Please. We need to leave."

I hurried into the hall and almost ran into Mr. Johnson. "I found my lens cap."

His eyes narrowed. "I thought you had to use the restroom."

"I do, but—"

"She was lost, just as you said." Abbie stood next to her husband. "It's the second door on your left from here."

"Thanks." I did a quick walk to the restroom, closed the door, and leaned my back against the raised-paneled wood. "That was close."

I took care of business and joined Morgan, who stood guard at the door. "Let's go home."

"That's the best plan you've had all day."

After collecting Ruthie and the dogs, we sped toward the studio, then hurried to the main office. Now was a good time to break and enter Mr. Johnson's office. I knew for a fact he wasn't there.

"Oh, good." Ruthie pulled a set of keys from her purse. "I snatched these from the foyer table when I was alone. I bet one of these keys fits the lock."

"You're a genius." I snatched the keys from her fingers. The fifth one fit. "We're in. Lock the door behind us."

I surveyed the plush waiting room before trying the handle on the door labeled Mr. Johnson. Locked, of course. Several tries with the keys and we were in. "Morgan, you keep watch. Ruthie can help me look. Don't make a mess." I shot her a sharp glance.

"I know better than that." She handed me a pair of vinyl gloves. "I always carry several pairs in my bag. You never know when they'll come in handy."

I snapped them over my hands and sat at Mr. Johnson's polished cherry-wood desk. The only filing cabinet in sight was the bottom drawer. None of the keys fit.

"Here." Ruthie handed me a bobby pin.

"They still make these?" Huh. I wiggled it around until a faint click signaled I'd succeeded. Sliding the bobby pin into my ponytail, I opened the drawer.

Several manila file folders filled the drawer. I

pulled them out and set them on the desk blotter. This would take some time.

Keeping the files in the order they were in, I flipped through each, snapping pictures with my phone of anything that looked interesting. Several financial reports showed promise, then bingo. A file of transactions between Mr. Johnson and Melanie's place. Okay, we know he owns the building. Who did he pay to keep their mouth shut?

"Gotta go." Morgan slapped the file closed. "Johnson just pulled into the parking lot."

I returned the files, closed and locked the drawer, then followed Morgan out a back door, pulling it shut as we heard a key turn in the front door lock. Too close for comfort.

We dashed to the van and peeled from the parking lot. "Yahoo!" I laughed and slapped the steering wheel.

"Girl, you're crazier than a fruit bat." Morgan shook his head. "You really get a thrill from all this, don't you?"

"I sure do." Maybe I was crazy, but I knew in my gut my cell phone held evidence to help crack this case.

At home I printed off the pictures of the files and carried my camera to my dark room at the back of the house. I developed Johnson's photos, setting aside the ones without him or his wife. The developed pictures would be ready for delivery on Monday.

When I'd finished, I carried what I needed to study to the kitchen table. Brock and Morgan ate pie and drank coffee. "Hey, guys." I set the photos on the table.

"We're working, I see." Brock stood and gave me a tender kiss. "I missed you."

"You weren't even gone a whole day." I smiled up at him. "But I missed you too." I got a slice of pie—cherry, my favorite—poured a mug of coffee, then joined the men. "Where's Ruthie?"

"Washing her fur ball." Morgan grimaced. "That dog is too hyper. Ruthie will be as wet as Sassy by the time she's finished." He reached over and fingered one of the photos of Johnson's home office.

I studied the ones of financial transactions. Several minutes later, I found something. I tapped my finger on the photo. "Money from Johnson's account is deposited to this one on a regular basis. I bet this is our dirty cop. How can we find out who the account belongs to?"

Morgan shrugged. "I don't know anyone who works at the bank. Maybe Lisa could find out."

Of course. Anything online was within her grasp. I texted her the account number.

Ten minutes later, my cell phone rang. "Tell me you have something."

"Not really," Lisa said. "It's an offshore account."

"Of course, it is." I gave her another account number. "This one is used a lot, too, but not as much as the other one."

The clicking of her fingers on the keys drifted through the air waves. "Ronald Warren."

My eyes widened, and I glanced from Brock to Morgan. "Call Lori and Banks. We have something." I thanked Lisa and hung up.

I kept the men in suspense until Lori and Banks arrived. Banks first, then Lori five minutes later. Ruthie, damp from washing Sassy, served them pie and coffee, then all three sat at the table and stared at me.

"Stop teasing us," Lori said. "Why did you call us out here?"

I filled them in on the day, then about calling Lisa. "It'll take more work to find out who the offshore account belongs to, but one of the accounts receiving regular deposits from Johnson belongs to Ronald Warren. Detective Warren, perhaps?"

"That's his name." Lori's eyes brightened. "This might not be enough proof to lock him up, but it's enough to warrant an investigation. Banks?" She turned to my brother.

He nodded. "I'll send it to someone higher up and not in our department. If the information goes to the wrong person, nothing will happen except alert them to the fact we're on to them. I don't want to increase the risk to any of us. Things are hot enough."

Excitement rippled through me. "We're getting close, guys. I feel it."

Brock put his arm around my shoulders and squeezed. "I think you're right. We're closing in."

"That's when things get hotter," Lori said. "You need to exercise more caution, Kelly. If this recent information gets out, the risk to you will escalate and you'll find yourself in heaven with your father."

The excitement fizzled out. I didn't want to die, but if by doing so, the person responsible for my father's death was caught, it would be worth the price. "Morgan is paid the big bucks to keep us safe."

"You don't pay me enough to cover the cost of some of the things you do. I swear you've given me more gray hairs in the last few weeks, then all my years before."

"Poor baby." I crossed my arms. "I'm going to see this through."

Brock sighed. "Just like you said the last time you almost got killed."

Chapter Eighteen

Instead of heading home after filming the next day, I drove us, despite protests, to Melanie's place. I did my best to park the van behind a large oleander bush, but I didn't hold on to hope that no one would notice. The van's green contrasted with the green of the plant leaves.

"I don't like this," Morgan said, scowling. "I'm here under large protest."

"We never see any sign of Warren at night. If he comes here, it might be during his work." I leaned forward and peered through the windshield.

"There's nothing to say he comes here at all," Morgan pointed out.

"True."

"I didn't see him when I was here the other day," Brock said.

I whipped around. "Why were you here?"

"To let Carly know she has an audition." His

eyes widened in innocence, then he wiggled his eyebrows. "I asked some more questions but didn't learn anything new, unfortunately."

I shrugged, shoving aside jealousy. I really wanted to know what this Carly looked like. She could quite possibly leave this job, if her acting was any good. I gasped. "If she works for Johnson, she knows too much. He might not let her leave here."

The van grew silent, then Ruthie said, "We need to get her out of there and hide her away until this is all over."

"Hold on." Morgan held up his hands. "We don't know that Johnson knows Carly has spoken to Brock."

"How else would she have an audition with Brock's agent after Brock visited a couple of times?" I shook my head. "Ruthie is right. Carly may be in danger. When is her audition?"

"Next week. Hey, isn't that the reporter, Susan Gilroy?" Brook flicked his thumb in the direction of the sidewalk.

Uh-oh. My one-time nemesis when I worked as paparazzi strolled in our direction with a large Great Dane.

The three dogs with us immediately bounded over Morgan. Sassy yapped louder than usual.

Morgan shoved at them. "Blasted dogs. I can't breathe."

Susan stopped and smiled. "Hello, Kelly. What in the world are you all doing?"

"Sitting." I tried to look nonchalant. "You?"

"I live down the street."

I perked up. "You do? Do you walk this way

often?"

"Every day. Why?" She narrowed her eyes.

"Know anything about that house?"

She glanced toward Melanie's place. "I think it's a group home."

"Nope." Ruthie snatched Sassy away from the window and clamped her hand around the dog's muzzle. "It's a whorehouse."

Susan looked stunned. "Are you sure?"

"Positive. Brock has been—"

Susan grinned. "Hollywood's Golden Boy has visited a whorehouse? This will make a great story."

I wanted to strangle my grandmother. "Not in that way. He's helping one of the girls get auditions."

"I bet." She laughed. "This is the best thing I've heard in a long time."

A muscle ticked in Brock's jaw. "I'm sure whatever you print will be a lie, but I can't stop you."

"Freedom of the press and all that." She wiggled her fingers. "See you idiots later." She sauntered off.

"If she writes that article, Carly will garner even more attention. You have to go get her, Brock." I unlocked the passenger door.

"Now?"

"Yes, now."

"How am I supposed to reach her without being seen?"

"You're a smart man. Figure it out. Oh, no. More trouble." Jerard and his entourage marched our way, then surrounded us.

Jerard leaned in the open driver's window. "You don't listen very well, Miss Canyon."

"We're here on a rescue mission," Ruthie said.

I seriously needed to duct tape her mouth. "We think one of the girls inside is in danger."

He stiffened. "Not Carly?"

"Yep, that's the one." Ruthie ran her fingers through Sassy's hair.

"That's my cousin. What's going on?"

I sighed and explained as little as I could, emphasizing that she might know too much for her own good. "Brock is headed in now to get her."

Jerard straightened. "See that three-story brick building down the street?"

I nodded, focusing on a run-down apartment complex.

"Bring her there. We'll take care of her."

"She has an audition next week," Brock said. "It could change her life."

"If she's out of danger, she'll be there." His eyes flashed. "Now go get her." He led his group away.

"I'll do my best." Brock exited the van. "This won't be easy."

With my heart in my throat, I watched him enter the house. Fifteen minutes later, he darted from the back of the house minus his tee shirt, his hand clutching that of a petite black girl. Morgan threw open the van door, and Carly dove inside.

"Thanks." The young girl smoothed down Brock's shirt.

"We're taking you to Jerard's." I floored the gas

pedal and squealed tires down the street. Not very subtle, but time was of the essence.

We slammed to a halt outside the building Jerard mentioned. He stood in the doorway and waved for us to come in.

"No," Morgan said.

"Come on. He won't hurt you." Carly climbed over the seat. "Believe me when I tell you that you want Jerard as a friend, not an enemy."

I couldn't agree more. I grabbed my camera bag as we climbed from the van, dogs and all, and followed Jerard into a hall that smelled of urine and mold. A baby cried from somewhere upstairs. How did people live like this?

I pasted on my acting face and followed Jerard up two flights of stairs. Of course, he lived on the top floor.

"Give the man back his shirt," Jerard ordered Carly. "You can find something of your own to wear in the bedroom."

She nodded and peeled off the shirt, wearing nothing but a pink negligee underneath. "Not out here!" Jerard muttered something under his breath. "No decency, Carly."

"Oh, you're one to talk." She stomped to a room off the small living space and returned a moment later wearing a yellow sundress. "I'll need some new clothes, Jerard. I got an audition."

"We'll talk about that later." He turned his attention back to us. "Thank you."

"How did she get started there?" I glanced at the young men and a couple of teenage girls lounging on torn and faded furniture.

"Not a lot of ways for a girl to make money in this hood." He stared at Brock. "She's a good girl. Make sure she gets the part she's auditioning for."

"I have no control over that. She can either act or she can't," Brock said.

"I can act." Carly sat cross-legged on the floor. "How do you think I acted like I enjoyed those men?"

She had a point there. "Why are we here, Jerard? We could have dropped her off and been on our way."

"You need to hide out for a while. You were attracting some unwanted attention. Look out the window."

We crowded around the one window. Another group of men stood on the opposite sidewalk, staring up at us.

"Who are they?"

"Rivals. They don't like when white people enter this neighborhood. You'd best wait them out. We've pizza in the kitchen and bottled water. You won't die of any disease if you stay awhile." He plopped onto a bean bag chair. A few Styrofoam pebbles, the kind used to fill these types of chairs, flew into the air.

"Hey, Canyon!" Someone yelled from the street below. "Can we have your autograph?"

I glanced at Jerard. "Maybe they're just fans."

"And maybe they ain't."

I opened the window. "Why don't just one of you come up and get it?"

"And get shot? No thanks."

I grabbed a napkin from the floor, dug around

the garbage for something to write with, then yelled back. "What's your name?"

"Damon."

I scribbled "to Damon with love, Kelly Canyon," then tossed the napkin out the window. It fluttered to the ground like a wounded butterfly.

He darted across the street to retrieve it, then waved it in the air. "Thanks, lady!" With a motion of his hand, he led his group away.

"See? Just fans." I grinned at the others.

"You got lucky this time," Jerard said, lighting a cigarette, then blowing a perfect smoke circle into the air. "You can go now."

"Gee, thanks." I rolled my eyes.

Shutterbug, as if sensing Carly's distress, had curled up next to her. I snapped my fingers, and she came with one last glance at the young girl.

"You're such a good dog." I patted her head.

Shutterbug's ears went up and she darted out the open door. Brutus followed while Sassy squirmed in Ruthie's arms.

I raced after the dogs. By the time I reached the bottom of the stairs, my breath came in painful gasps. "Shutterbug. Stop."

My dog ceased her mad chase just inside the doorway. Brutus collided into her but continued to bark at something across the street. I took one step outside.

Something hit the van.

Pea-green parts exploded and filled the air, knocking me backward into the stairwell banister.

When I came to, I stared up into Brock's face. "I'd been hoping someone would blow that ugly thing up."

He laughed and sat next to me, cradling my head in his lap. "Police are coming. Do you need an ambulance?"

"I'm not sure. I'll let you know when I don't feel like I'm dying."

"That sounds like a yes to me," Ruthie said, bending over me. "Morgan, call an ambulance."

Sirens wailed, then faded outside the building. Warren and Banks strode into the building.

"What are you doing here?" Warren glared.

"Nice to see you too." I pushed to a sitting position, every inch of me screaming. "Call it research. Oh, and I signed an autograph."

"It's always research to you." His face darkened. He glanced to the second landing where Jerard and his homies peered down. "You the ones that called the police?"

Jerard nodded. "Reluctantly. But, she came to us to find out how the other side lives. For a book she said."

Bless that boy for confirming my story. "Someone blew up the van," I said.

"Really?" Warren glanced at me as if I were a bug. A stupid bug at that. "She needs her head checked. Probably hit it hard."

Considering the blood running down my neck, that was a positive assessment. I leaned against Brock and waited for medical attention.

"You got here fast." I glared up at Warren.

"We were in the neighborhood."

I just bet he was. Through the open doorway, I could see firemen spraying the flaming van with a hose. "Where's my camera bag?"

Morgan handed it to me. "Found it in the corner."

I glanced inside, relieved to see that nothing looked broken. I'd upgraded to an expensive, padded camera case with my first acting advance. You get what you pay for.

"It looks like a pipe bomb," Banks said, casting a quick glance at me over Warren's shoulder. "You okay?"

I nodded.

Paramedics entered, forcing Warren and Brock outside and tended to the cut on my head. I refused to be taken to the hospital. "It's nothing more than a concussion, and not my first one."

"Concussions are dangerous," the male paramedic said.

"I'll go if I get worse." I held up my hand for Brock to help me to my feet. After a second on wobbly legs, I stood steady. "Home sounds like the best bet. We'll need a ride."

"I called Uber," Morgan said. "Two of them."

We stepped outside. I blinked against the harsh afternoon sun and glanced up at the third-story window. Warren followed my gaze.

Looking down at us was the pretty face of Carly.

"Concussions aren't the only dangerous thing, Canyon," Warren said, his jaw taut. "Sticking your nose where it doesn't belong is far more so."

Chapter Nineteen

Brock, myself, and our two dogs crowded into one Uber, while Morgan, Ruthie, and Sassy took the other. When we arrived home, Lori waited on the front porch.

"Banks called me," she said. "I guess you have some things to tell me."

"Inside." Morgan gripped her by the arm and dragged her in the house. "Kelly has managed to escalate the danger in her own special way."

I headed straight for the bathroom medicine cabinet and popped a couple of ibuprofen while the others filled Lori in on our day. When I rejoined them, every head turned in my direction.

"What?"

"Warren threatened you?" Lori's brows lowered. "He just happened to be in the area where your van blew up?"

"He and Banks. I don't think my brother would

try to kill me." Although I didn't know him well, I felt I could trust him.

"No, but it wouldn't be hard for Warren to slip away and hire someone else. Most of the dirty work has been done by punks." She paced the room. "You aren't safe in a group of people. How do you manage that feat? And this Carly? He knows where she is. I'm going to have to get her out and hope I don't get shot in the process."

"I had no intention of doing anything other than catching Warren entering the house." I fell onto the sofa. "Everything else just happened. I also don't think Warren hired Jerard or Damon to harm me."

"Who's Damon?"

"Some kid I gave an autograph to. A rival gang member, I think." I closed my eyes and concentrated on my breathing. Maybe I should have gone to the hospital. My head ached worse than it ever had.

Someone placed a cool rag on my forehead. I opened my eyes and stared into Brock's gorgeous face. "You're so sweet."

"I'd take away the pain if I could."

"I know." I smiled and let him care for me.

The tapping of Lori's shoes as she paced sounded like anvils on iron to me. She ranted and raved as she moved, sometimes muttering. I preferred the muttering. Finally, she stopped. "No more taking the dogs. If you hadn't chased after them, you wouldn't have gotten injured."

"Shutterbug heard something."

"I don't care. Regardless of what you may think, Kelly, you are not qualified for this."

My eyes popped open. "You can't make me stop. You're suspended."

"I can still advise you." She put her hands on her hips. "The rest of you need to convince her to back off and let me handle this."

"By yourself?" I sat up. "It takes more than one person to do this."

"I want to catch my father's killer. I'm his daughter, you were only a girlfriend." I regretted the words the moment they left my mouth. Her face fell and she covered her face with her hands. I hurried to her. "I'm sorry. I know we both want this. I didn't mean it." I'd grown to care for my father's last love and would never hurt her feelings on purpose.

"I know." She exhaled as if the world's weight rested on her shoulders. "I'm frustrated. We're going nowhere fast."

"We know Warren is involved. That's something." If only Lisa could find out who owned the offshore account.

"Let's take the afternoon off," Ruthie suggested. "Actually, more like early evening. Let's go to the beach and let the waves wash away our cares." She flung her arms wide for emphasis.

"That sounds wonderful," I said. Lying in the sand and listening to the waves would do wonders for my head. "Except I'm supposed to take Johnson his pictures."

"We'll stop on the way home. That won't take but a couple of minutes. You can toss the envelope on the porch as we drive by." Ruthie clapped her hands. "We leave in fifteen minutes."

Since we loved the beach so much, we kept beach bags, dog treats and toys, and easy food fixings ready and waiting. Now that the ugly van was no more, we had to take several vehicles. Ruthie still put the kibosh on taking the Thunderbird, so Brock and I squeezed into my Volkswagen with Shutterbug and Brutus crammed into the backseat, leaving Morgan, Ruthie, and Sassy to ride with Lori.

"You need to buy a bigger vehicle," Brock said, buckling his seatbelt. "An SUV or something. Brutus barely fits in this little car."

"Not my fault. I love this car."

He placed a tender kiss on my cheek. "Remember when we used to be able to go places alone? I miss those days."

"Me too." We hadn't had a good necking session in a long time. "Maybe we can sneak away while the others play in the water." I smiled.

"I'll do my darndest to make that happen. If nothing else, we can hide behind that big umbrella we're taking."

My skin tingled at the touch.

The sun hung low in the sky by the time we found a spot we liked on Huntington. The temperature had dropped several degrees, making me glad for the multiple beach towels Ruthie always insisted on bringing.

Morgan dragged Ruthie away almost immediately. They walked down the shore, barefoot, hand-in-hand.

"Go away, Lori," Brock said. "Unless you like to watch folks kiss." He bent the umbrella as low as possible, shielding us from those along the water's edge.

"Not fair." Lori padded away.

Brock leaned over and pressed his lips against mine. As our kiss intensified, he stretched alongside me, shifting me to face him. His hand ran up my leg and over my hip. I forgot all about the knock to the head as my body responded to his touch and kiss.

His lips moved to my neck. I closed my eyes.

"Well, Mr. Brock Hanson does get around."

My eyes snapped open. Brock kept me close despite my struggle to move away.

"Go away, Susan." The flash of her camera blinded me.

"From whorehouse to beach blanket. The halo falls from the head of Hollywood's Golden Boy." She grinned. "How do you like the title?"

"Why are you so mean?" I glared.

"Just making a living. You know as well as I do that readers love to see celebrities fall. See ya." She sauntered off, tightening the floral sarong she wore around her waist.

"I really don't like that woman."

"Hmm." Brock resumed his nuzzling.

"Doesn't it bother you? The article she's going to write?"

"No," he muttered in the space where my shoulder connected to my neck. "Forget her. My fans won't believe her lies. If they do, it's good publicity for me. Now, hush. The others won't stay gone long."

I relaxed and enjoyed his kisses, savoring a moment of normality between us, until Morgan and Ruthie poked their heads under the umbrella and made kissy sounds. "Morgan is hungry," Ruthie said, grinning like a child caught spying on his sister and her boyfriend.

Brock groaned and buried his face in the towel he lay on. "This group is impossible."

"If you moved in with us, you'd have lots of time together," Ruthie said, tossing him an apple.

"Nope." He took a big bite. "Not until I'm at least engaged to the woman."

Oh, how I hoped someday I would be 'the woman,' I peeled a banana. "Where's Lori?"

"Here. Banished like an unwanted child." She folded up the umbrella.

"You need a man, dear." Ruthie handed her a ham and cheese sandwich.

Lori eyed it warily. "Don't you bring all pre-prepared food?"

"Not the sandwiches." Ruthie looked shocked. "I brought bread, ham, and cheese. I always keep little packets of condiments in the kitchen drawer. It only takes a minute to grab."

"Good." Lori bit into her sandwich as if she hadn't eaten all day. "I'm starving. I don't need a man, just food."

"No, you need a man." Morgan sat down. "I've got the woman I've always wanted. Your turn."

Tears sprang to her eyes. "The man I always wanted was shot down in the street."

The banana caught in my throat. While I, too,

sought vengeance, ten years was a long time. Too long for a pretty woman like Lori to remain single.

"When Kevin's killer is caught, then I might consider opening my heart again." She reached for an apple. "Until then, drop the subject."

Brock jumped to his feet and pulled me up to join him. "Do you think you can handle a short stroll?"

"Yes." The pounding in my head had ebbed and a walk in the surf with Brock sounded wonderful. I toed off my sandals and skipped to the water's edge. Sometimes, Ruthie had the best ideas. Like every time she suggested a trip to the beach.

My toes sank deeper with every lap of the silver-tipped waves. I didn't think a person could get any closer to heaven than the beach at sunset. The two larger dogs splashed in the waves while Sassy sat like a little priss far enough away not to get wet.

I stood with Brock's arm around my waist for a few minutes until Morgan called to me that Ruthie had reminded him about filming in the morning. I sighed and cupped Brock's face. Staring into his eyes, I almost told him I loved him, but I bit back the words, although I wasn't sure why.

He leaned his forehead against mine. "I know," he whispered before he kissed me one last time. Not one of passion like before but one full of sweet emotion.

"Let's go!" Morgan yelled.

Brock chuckled. "We timed that just right. They've folded everything up."

We filled our arms with beach stuff and trudged

back to the parking lot. "Don't forget that I have to drop off Johnson's photos," I told the others. "Brock and I will follow shortly."

Lori gave a thumbs-up and pulled out of the parking lot. Seconds later, Brock and I followed, turning off at the exit we needed. I laid my head back against the seat, content to let someone else drive for a change.

"We're here." Brock shook me awake. "I can drop off the photos if you want. Where are they?"

"Under my seat." I blinked a few times and pulled the large envelope from its hiding place. "I'll be right back." I shoved open my door, raced to the front door, and started to leave the envelope on the doormat but stopped.

The front door was open a couple of inches. Strange. "Hello?" I pushed it open further. "Mr. Johnson? Abbie?"

The house was dark. I held one finger up to Brock.

"No way, Kelly." He climbed from the car. "Do not go inside."

I pretended not to hear. Nothing looked out of the ordinary in the foyer. In fact, a new set of keys sat on the small marble-topped table. The moon glimmering through the wall of windows provided enough light for me to see that nothing looked ransacked.

"I guess they just forgot to lock the door." I set the photos on the foyer table. "I'll call tomorrow and tell him where the pictures are." Good thing I take payment up front.

"Then, let's go." Brock seized my hand.

"It's the perfect opportunity to search the study in more depth."

"No."

The back door stood ajar. Even with the cool evening, it seemed strange that two doors would be open and no one at home. "Just a minute. Something doesn't seem right."

My footsteps made no sound as I hurried across the plush carpet. I stepped onto the patio and down the three stairs to the pool.

Floating face up was Abbie Johnson, her bikini top wrapped around her neck.

Chapter Twenty

"What is going on here?" Johnson and his goon Harrelson, both wet and wearing thick cotton robes, stepped onto the patio. Johnson glanced at the water. "Abbie!"

He bounded toward the pool, jumped in, and scooped his wife into his arms. "Harrelson, help me."

The bigger man took the woman's lifeless form and laid her on a pool chaise. His rock-hard face conveyed no emotion.

Johnson spun toward me. "You did this. You killed my Abbie."

"No." I stepped back, putting my hands up. "I have no reason to want her dead."

"Call the police, Harrelson. Funny that Miss Canyon is here alone, standing over my wife's dead body."

"I'm not even wet!"

Harrelson took care of that and shoved me into the pool. I came up sputtering. "You're framing me?"

Warren and Banks, with Brock on their heels, sprinted toward the pool from the house. Brock leaned over and offered me his hand. "What happened?" he whispered.

"Arrest these two, Detective, for the murder of my love." He fell to his knees, suddenly the epitome of a grieving husband. Laying a towel over his wife's nudeness, he pointed a finger at me. "I caught this woman standing over Abbie's body."

Brock pulled me from the water and handed me a nearby towel. Knowing it would be no use, I turned to Warren. "I came to deliver Mr. Johnson's photos and found the front door open. I called out, and when nobody answered, I came out here and found…Abbie."

"Witnesses?" Warren's eyes glittered.

"No, I told you no one answered!" Shudders overtook me and I collapsed onto a lounge chair. Warren was going to haul me to jail where I would be at his mercy or the mercy of some other dirty cop. "Brock, take care of Shutterbug for me."

"That's going to be tough for him to do from jail," Warren said. "I'm taking you both in on suspicion of murder. Banks, cuff them."

"I'll drop your dog off at your grandmother's," Bank said as he placed the restraints on my wrists. He lowered his voice. "I'll get you and Brock out as soon as I can. Keep your wits about you. This can't be good."

Once I was cuffed, he moved to Brock. Warren

looked more pleased than I'd ever seen the sour-faced detective. Morgan was going to blow his lid when he found out about my latest mishap.

Brock and I sat side by side while the medical examiner arrived and other officers cased the crime scene. I glared at Johnson who happened to be a poor actor, by the way. Anyone with half an eye could see he wasn't the least bit distraught over the loss of his wife.

After what seemed like forever, with the cell phone in my pocket vibrating for the hundredth time, they loaded us into the back of a squad car.

"The car keys are in the ignition," I told Banks. "If Shutterbug acts aggressive, say the word *hinunter*. It means 'down' in German. Say *Angriff* if you're in trouble and need her to attack. What is your first name?"

"Jason." He gave a quick nod and closed the door. I really hoped we could trust him as Lori felt we could. I'd hate to find a brother, then discover he was one of the very crooks we tried to take down.

"Your halo sure is getting tarnished lately," I told Brock, choking back tears. "I'm so sorry. I hope I don't cause you to be less sought after for starring roles."

"You won't be. I'd rather get them based on my talent any old day." He leaned his head against the back of the seat. "I've never been arrested before. My mom is going to kill me."

"Stick around with me long enough and you'll experience a lot of firsts."

Warren slid into the driver's seat, still looking as happy as a kid at the fair. We sat silent as he drove us to the police station and booked us. I almost said, "Book 'em, Dano," but didn't think that would go over well considering the circumstances.

Brock and I were put into holding cells side by side. I could see him, but the window between us prevented conversation. The handcuff, now attached between my wrist and the metal stool bolted to the ground, kept me from moving. It was going to be a long night.

Hopefully when Banks took Shutterbug home and explained to Ruthie, she'd come bail me out. I leaned my head against the concrete wall and closed my eyes to wait.

A tapping on the grated window woke me up. "Kelly."

"Ruthie. Are you here to bail me out?"

"That twerp, Warren, said I can't until a judge signs off that you aren't a danger to others." Tears welled in her eyes. "He's letting Brock go, though. I'm frightened something will happen to you."

She wasn't the only one. If I still breathed in this cell come morning, I might have a chance of seeing another twenty-four hours. "I'll be fine. Please figure out a way to get me out. Don't you know any judges from your…uh…exotic days?" Certainly, she must have met a judge, or at least a politician, during her former career days. That's where she met Morgan.

"I'm not sure." She tapped a manicured finger against her lips. "They may not want to admit they used to frequent those types of places."

"No worse than Melanie's place."

"True." Tears spilled down her cheeks. "I love you. Keep your chin up. Oh..." She pulled something from inside her bra and tossed it at my feet. "Swallow that."

"It came out of your bra!"

"It's a tracker," she hissed. "Morgan said you have to swallow it. We'll know where you are for seventy-two hours. Do it."

Where did the man find these things? I stretched as far as I could and lifted the small silver disc with two fingers. Forcing back the thought of where Ruthie had stashed it, I popped it into my mouth like an aspirin and swallowed.

Seconds later, Warren sauntered in and told Ruthie she had to leave. He flashed me a feral grin and escorted her away.

I wanted to yell after them. Demand to be released. Talk to a lawyer. Somehow, I didn't think Warren would act very quickly on any of those requests.

I gave into tears and stared at a spot on the floor, refusing to think of what body fluid had caused it. When I'd cried myself dry, I leaned back and forced my eyes shut again.

If someone did come for me, I'd need to be rested with as many wits about me as I could muster, since I might very well have to fight my way to freedom. Thank goodness I'd studied self-defense in preparation for the part I played in our TV series. No way in Hades would I go down without a fight.

Oh, please someone let me out of here. I felt as if someone was watching me and opened my eyes to see Warren staring in at me, then he smirked and walked away. He'd regret the day he messed with Kelly Canyon.

I must have fallen asleep again because the next thing I knew, an officer I'd never met set a tray with a bologna sandwich and a bottle of water next to me. "Thanks." I took the water and left the sandwich.

The young officer actually snarled at me. I hadn't realized how many people were in Johnson's pocket, or pretended to be. Wait. He dropped something near the leg of my chair.

The officer wasn't in Johnson's pocket. He'd dropped a handcuff key. Could it be a trap? Which was riskier…take my chances here waiting for Warren or use the key and try to escape? I chose escape.

Less than a minute later, I was free. Moving slow enough not to make any noise, I placed my hand on the door and pushed. It opened on well-oiled hinges. With my heart in my throat, I glanced both ways. Could I really walk out of jail?

No one sat behind the glass in front of the desk where Warren had checked me in. The door under a glowing exit sign stood open enough for me to see the lure of moonlight. With a glance behind me, I made a run for it, slamming the door open further and dashing across the parking lot.

Where could I go? Not home. Warren would look there first. The studio was also off limits. Oh, Lord, I was a fugitive from the law.

I stopped and sagged against a closed shop wall and brought a hand to my chest. Me, the daughter of

Detective Kevin Canyon, fleeing from the authorities for a crime I didn't commit. Sounded like every police thriller ever filmed.

The tracker. I put a hand to my stomach. Find a place to hide and Lori would come for me. I dashed down an alley, then another. I knew this neighborhood.

Before I could change my mind, I raced for Jerard's building and up the stairs. I stopped in front of his apartment and banged on the door.

It swung open. Someone shoved a gun in my face just seconds before yanking me into the room.

"Are you crazy?" Jerard scowled. "I almost shot you. It's never good for white people to bang on a brother's door at this hour."

"You've got to hide me." I placed my palms on my knees and struggled to catch my breath. "I just escaped from jail. They won't think to look for me here."

"I don't need any more trouble, lady," he said, setting the gun on the table. "I've already got enough. What did you do?"

"Nothing. They booked me on suspicion of murder. I think they planned on killing me to shut me up." I straightened. "Are you going to help me or not?"

"You're killing me, lady." He snapped his fingers at Carly who slept on the sofa. "Go get Lars."

She jumped up and disappeared into the bedroom, returning a few minutes later with a scrawny teenage boy.

"What?" He scowled at me.

"Take this woman to Douglas."

"Man, this is the first time in two days I got to stretch out. Can't someone else do it?"

"I told you to do it." Jerard gave him a shove to the door. "Don't be seen. The cops are after her."

"Great." Lars hitched up his low-hanging jeans. "I'm going to end up in jail again because of some white woman."

"A very appreciative white woman." I forced a smile. "Shall we go?" I turned back to Jerard. "Thank you."

"I'll come to you for a favor when I need one. Nothing comes free, lady." He nodded for Lars to take me away.

Lars led me up one street and down another until I had no idea where I was. If I asked a question, he told me to shut my mouth. I took a gulp from the water bottle I'd been smart enough to snag and hurried to catch up.

"Can we slow down a little?"

"Nope." He pushed an iron gate open, which squeaked on rusty hinges. "You cannot tell a single person where we are. If you do, we're both dead."

"Who am I going to tell? The cops took my cell phone. I am thoroughly lost and dependent on gang members." What a book I'd have to write if I made it out of this alive.

We climbed a set of cement stairs and stopped in front of a door with chipped green paint. Lars knocked and announced his name. "Jerard sent a package."

The door opened on a dark room. An obese man sat in a chair in the corner, a semi-automatic weapon lying across his lap. "This had better be good, kid since you're here in the middle of the night." The man stood and waddled into what little light shone through the window.

He narrowed his eyes at me. "What's your name?"

"Am I supposed to tell you?" I glanced at Lars.

The boy nodded.

"Kelly Canyon."

"Get her out of here!" The man roared and aimed the gun. "Her father is the one who locked me up for ten years. I lost everything."

I didn't need to be told twice. I turned tail and ran as the doorframe exploded behind me.

Chapter Twenty-One

I hurtled over an overturned trash can on my way out of the building. Where could I go with no money, no phone…nothing? At least I had my gym shoes and could run. I veered left, further away from the police station.

Thankfully, at two a.m., the streets were mostly deserted. A woman alone on the fringes of Compton skirted a razor-thin edge of safety. How long until Lori followed the tracker inside me?

What if it didn't work? My steps faltered. I might be out here alone for who knows how long. I glanced at the few swallows left of my water bottle and knew I needed to find a place to hide and soon.

In time, although I wasn't sure how much, I stumbled upon a homeless community. Wary glances were cast my way as I shuffled among the cardboard homes and discarded shopping carts. A faint scent of seawater let me know I wasn't too far from a beach. I'd run farther than I'd thought. I kept going, ignoring a pair of drunken hands reaching out for me, until I reached sand and collapsed under a dock.

I felt pretty sure no one would think to look for me this far from home. They might question Jerard, but even he didn't know where I'd gone.

Why had no one come for me? I sat on the damp sand, wrapped my arms around my knees to help stop the shivering, and gave into the tears.

Maybe I didn't have what it took to find Dad's killer. The person had gotten away with it for ten years. Always one step ahead of me.

"Hey." A woman wearing two coats removed one and held it out to me. "You look cold."

"I am. Thank you." I draped the musty-smelling garment around my shoulders and wore it as if it were the finest cloak.

"You're that actress, Kelly Canyon." She sat next to me. "What's wrong?"

The price of fame. You couldn't go anywhere without someone knowing your name. "Someone is trying to kill me."

"Are you filming a movie?" She glanced around us.

"No, this is for real."

She gripped my arm. "Come on. I have a place for you. It isn't much, but no one will think of looking for a movie star under a bridge."

True. I pushed to my feet and trudged after her.

The bridge wasn't more than a concrete culvert in the road. "What do you do when it rains?"

She looked at me as if I'd grown three horns. "I

move if water starts coming in. See those?" She pointed to a couple of plastic bins. "I have all my belongings in those. I'm not a bag lady; I'm a bin lady." She laughed at her turn of a phrase.

Okay then. Leaves, rocks, and paper covered the bottom of the wide concrete tunnel, muffling our footsteps and keeping us from sitting on the ground. Not the Ritz, but not bad. My new friend was right. No one would think of searching for me here. "What's your name?"

"Sarah." She dug in one of the bins and brought out a package of peanut butter crackers. "Here. You need to eat. I'm not like those other people. When someone gives me money, I buy food and bottled water."

"Good for you and thank you." I tore into the package. When all this was behind me, I'd find Sarah and give her more money than she'd ever dreamed of. "What made you become homeless?"

"A cheating husband, a high mortgage, and forced early retirement." She sat across from me and opened her own package of crackers. "I barely worked. He preferred me at home so what little social security I get doesn't pay for much. Keeps food in my belly, well, that and the local soup kitchen."

"No family?"

"God never blessed us with children. I am truly alone."

"Not anymore." I put my hand over hers. "Can you cook?"

She nodded. "I took some culinary classes before I got married but quit before finishing. I can read a recipe like nobody else can." She flashed another grin.

"Good." I found a broken pencil near my feet and wrote Ruthie's address on a piece of paper. "Go here and tell Ruthie Canyon that I sent you. She's looking for a chef."

"Well now, I can't do that until you're no longer in danger, can I?" She smiled. "I've got time. If the job is still open in a week or so, I'll consider knocking on her door. But I won't accept the job unless she likes my cooking. No charity accepted here."

"You're one smart woman, Sarah."

"I've learned to be cautious. Why do you think I'm here instead of in the homeless community? A lot of riffraff in there will steal you blind."

"Where's your husband now?"

"Married to some bimbo in Beverly Hills." She spit on the ground.

"What's his name?"

She narrowed her eyes. "Why?"

I smiled. "I might just pay him a visit and tell him a thing or two."

"His name is Richard Doles. Bigshot corporate man who married his secretary. Didn't have enough imagination not be a cliché."

"You should have received alimony."

"I just wanted out. That was fifteen years ago and water under the bridge, ha! I'm full of them."

I finished the crackers and the last of my water, then lay down to sleep, warm in the pungent coat. I'd make Doles pay up or suffer the embarrassment of his colleagues knowing what kind of a guy he was.

Sarah's kindness brought tears to my eyes. She didn't deserve this kind of life. With so little and yet without a moment of hesitation, she shared what she had with me, a woman with a very large bank account. When I could come out of hiding, I'd make sure she never lived as a homeless person again.

"You want to make a phone call?"

I jerked up. "You have a cell phone?"

"One of them Obama phones that he had the government hand out. I've a few minutes left. No one for me to call. Just don't stay on long enough for the call to be traced." She handed me a black flip phone.

"You watch a lot of movies."

"Out here?" She chuckled. "No, but I do have a library card."

I sat up. "You're an angel in disguise. You have to be." I dialed Lori's number.

"Lori Lawrence."

"It's Kelly. Don't say my name. I'm fine. Is the tracker working?"

"Yes, I don't need any insurance. Thank you. My agent was here just a few minutes ago."

"Warren is there?"

"Yes, sir. Have a good day. I'll let you know when I'm in the market for a new agent." Click.

I handed the phone back to Sarah. Lori was under watch. Which meant Ruthie and Brock were, as well. They'd come for me when they could. I prayed it would be within the seventy-two hours the tracker worked.

"Why is someone after you, if you don't mind

me asking?" Sarah stretched out.

I did the same, resuming my prior position. "I'm getting too close to pinning a murder on them."

"That would do it. Why?"

"Why what?"

"Why get involved?"

"I think these people had something to do with the murder of my father." I folded my arm under my head.

"Then I hope you send them to jail." She closed her eyes and started snoring.

It took me a little longer, but I did fall asleep until the rising sun shone on my face. I groaned and pushed to a sitting position. Despair weighed on my shoulders. I'd hoped to wake up to see Brock's handsome face peering down at me.

"Put this on." Sarah tossed me a knit hat. "And smear some dirt on your face. We're headed to the soup kitchen. Today is biscuits and gravy. It won't do for someone to recognize you."

I almost said I wouldn't go, but my growling stomach answered for me. I scooped up some mud and smeared some on my face.

"Not that much. We want you to blend into the background not make a spectacle of yourself." Sarah spit on a dirty rag and wiped most of the mud off.

I wasn't quite sure how to act to a relative stranger wiping my face with her spit. "Uh, thanks."

"Come on." She motioned her arm.

"Your stuff."

"No one will bother it."

I shrugged and stepped from our shelter into the

bright morning sun. Never in a million years would I have thought I'd see this side of life. But I still breathed, I still walked, I could still think. I would get through this.

The phone in Sarah's bag rang. She glanced at the number, then answered. "Yeah? Yep." She handed the phone to me. "She said her name is Lori."

"Thank you, God." I snatched the phone. "Are you coming?"

"As soon as I can. Stay safe. They're after you." Click.

I smiled through my tears and returned the phone to Sarah. "They're coming to get me."

"Good. Let's eat while you wait."

We left the beach and walked a few blocks to a run-down church. A line stretched out one door with people leaving another door with paper bowls of biscuits and gravy. My stomach growled more loudly.

"Live here long enough and you get used to being hungry," Sarah said, patting me on the back. "Keep your head down. Don't look at anyone."

I didn't think I could have found a better rescuer than this woman. We joined the line. For the first time in my life I prayed the food wouldn't run out before I received some. I'd have to do something in the future to help the homeless in this area. There were way too many people living without a roof over their head and full bellies.

When my turn came, I held out my hands to accept the food. I kept my head down, mumbled a thanks, and swiveled to go.

"You're new," the server said.

I nodded and kept moving, my heart in my throat. I hunched my shoulders and did everything I could not to be noticed. If Warren discovered me with these people, he wouldn't hesitate to make me disappear. What was one less homeless person?

Sarah led me to the shade of a palm tree away from the others. "Eat fast. You're attracting attention."

I glanced up to see several curious faces turned our way. "It's only because I'm new. They'll forget about me as soon as I'm out of sight."

"Maybe." She ate fast, then tossed her dishes into a nearby trash can. "You're too slow, girl. Come on."

I glanced up to see two uniformed officers coming our way. I tossed the rest of my food in the garbage, wrapped my arms around my middle, and shuffled after Sarah. Once we turned the corner out of sight, I straightened, and we increased our pace, not relaxing until we reached the culvert.

"You stay here," she ordered. "I need to do my daily scrounging. It's too dangerous."

"What if I'm picked up before you come back?" I gripped her hand. "How can I ever thank you enough?"

"I have the number you gave me. We'll meet again. I promise." She pulled free. "Stay safe, Kelly Canyon, and give thanks every day for what you have."

"You're at the top of the list, Sarah." Tears blurred my vision.

She wiped her nose on her sleeve and ducked

out of the culvert.

I shed the coat and draped it over one of the plastic bins, wishing I had money on me to leave her. Seeing the two police officers showed me I couldn't stay and endanger Sarah. With one last glance at my unlikely sanctuary, I headed in the opposite direction of my ragged angel.

Chapter Twenty-two

I had no destination in mind. I just walked. Knowing the tracker inside me worked, Lori, Morgan or someone would find me.

The closer I got to my father's killer, the more dangerous my life became. The poor maintenance man, murdered in the theater, might receive justice, might not. If Warren was the dirty cop, he'd hired someone to shoot Ruthie. The man didn't do any of his own dirty work. That had been proven.

I rounded a corner and came face-to-face with a group of young men I hadn't seen before. They weren't with Jerard or Damon. I started to turn around when they circled me, cutting off my escape.

"Got any money?" The lead, a young man who looked part Hispanic, stepped closer. "I sure hope so because the last person who didn't have any to give us found himself dead."

My throat clogged. It wouldn't do any good to

tell them I was broke and on the run. They'd kill me or beat me regardless. I turned in a slow circle scanning the area for an escape.

Morgan, gun aimed at the group, stepped into sight. "Back away, boys."

The leader laughed. "You going to shoot us all, old man?"

"How about I shoot you first?" Morgan motioned for me to come close. "Then I'll pick the others at random."

Big Talker held up his hands and backed away. "We were just having some fun." They pivoted and headed in the opposite direction.

I threw my arms around Morgan. "How did you know it was me?"

"Because of the mud?" He grinned. "You were wearing those clothes when Warren arrested you."

I glanced at the frayed denim, purposely distressed and expensive, and the stained tee shirt. "Right. Are you taking me home?"

"If the second shift of officers hasn't arrived yet. We have to hurry. You can tell us of your experiences once we get home." He gripped my arm and ran to a plain dark-green sedan. "Borrowed."

"You stole it?"

"Borrowed. From a neighbor. Another reason to return it quick." He opened the back door. "Get in and stay down."

"You took the car without Mrs. Pickles' knowledge."

"Hush." He slammed the door and slid into the driver's seat. Seconds later, he sped away.

My limbs loosened, and I relaxed. While I'd

managed to sleep in that culvert, the hard ground wasn't the most comfortable. My eyes closed and didn't open again until the car stopped. I peered out the window. Morgan parked the car in Mrs. Pickles' driveway.

"Stay low. You'll have to scale some fences."

"You do know how far apart these big houses are, right?" We'd be running for a while.

"Yes, but we have to stay out of sight of the road. I'll toss you over. Head to the house to the east. Brock will meet you there." He shoved me through an open backyard fence.

"Where are you going?"

"I went for a jog. I have to go back that way. Go." He gave me a push and dashed away.

"Alone again." I sighed and hurried in the direction he'd told me to go, more than eager to feast my eyes on Brock.

Morgan might have found it easy to climb over six-foot or higher fences, but me…not so much. Hoping to avoid being seen by the home's residents, I dragged a glass top coffee table to the fence and climbed up and over, falling into an oleander bush. Great. I had to land in a poisonous bush.

Climbing out, II dashed across the yard, squeezed through a side gate, used a trash can as a stepping stool, dove over another fence, and landed on a soft lawn.

Brock pulled me to my feet. After giving me a quick hug, he gripped my hand as we raced across the yard. Once he'd boosted me over yet another fence, he scaled up after me like the friendly neighborhood Spiderman.

When we finally ended up in my backyard, he drew me to him and gave me a kiss full of fear, raw emotion, and love. When he came up for air, Brock cupped my face in his hands and stared into my eyes. "I've never been more scared in my life. Where were you?"

"I'll explain it all after I shower, okay?" I caressed his face.

He nodded. "Yeah, you do smell a bit earthy." His mouth twitched.

"You have no idea." We entered through the back door where Lori, Ruthie, and a sweaty Morgan greeted us. Shutterbug raced from the kitchen and almost broke a rib from shaking her tail hard enough to almost bend her in half. She whined deep in her throat.

I knelt and hugged her neck. "I missed you too, girl."

"Stay away from all windows. We cannot let the authorities know you're here," Morgan ordered as he headed down the hall.

"Yes, sir!" I gave him a salute, begged the others to give me fifteen minutes, then hurried to my bedroom. I dropped the dirty clothes into a hamper and stepped into the shower with water as hot as I could stand.

When I felt human again and dressed in a comfy pair of yoga pants and a tank top, I rejoined the others in the living room. I plopped onto the sofa with Shutterbug at my feet and accepted the offered mug of coffee from Ruthie.

"Now spill," she said.

"Who set up my escape from jail?" I glanced at

Lori.

"Banks. He's the only one who had access to the building. Warren has had the rest of us under guard since your arrest. I received a text earlier telling me you were on the run, so I had Lisa trace it to a burner phone. I guess that was Banks' doing too."

I grinned. "I think I like having a brother who is also a cop."

The doorbell rang.

I shot off the sofa, told Shutterbug to stay, and darted into the closest room, the laundry. Where to hide?

"Where is she?" Warren's voice boomed.

"Who?" Ruthie asked.

"Your granddaughter. Someone helped her escape from jail."

"You've had this house watched," Brock said. "We haven't seen her since you took her from Johnson's house."

"I guess we'll have to take a look."

Yikes. I folded myself into the dryer and closed the door. Sometimes there were perks to being petite.

An officer, only his legs in view, passed the dryer. I held my breath, releasing it when his legs moved back out. I didn't know how long it took for them to search the house and determine I wasn't here, but my body cramped into position.

"Okay," Brock called.

I pushed the door open and fell onto the tiled floor. To be honest, falling grew old very fast. I pushed painfully to my feet and hobbled into the front room. "We need a bigger dryer."

My family and friends burst into laughter.

"I think we're safe for a while," Morgan said, tossing a towel over his shoulder. "Not the best thing to see when getting out of the shower…Warren."

"I can imagine. Sit, and I'll tell you of my adventures." I resumed my seat on the sofa.

"Jerard helped, but the man he sent me to tried to kill me. It appears that Dad sent him to jail once upon a time." I told them of breaking down on the beach and of Sarah finding me. How she kept me safe and fed me. "I told her to hunt you up, Ruthie, when this was all over. She has some culinary experience."

Ruthie wiped away tears. "I don't care whether she can only boil water, I'll give that angel a job because she took care of my baby." She wrapped her arms around me.

"I'll never assume homeless people are lazy," I said. "Maybe some of them are, and a few others scam people for money, but some just fall on bad times like Sarah." I left out her ex-husband's last name. That was something I wanted to handle myself. "What I need now is my bed."

Brock held out his hand. "I'll take you."

I slid my hand into his and let him lead me to my room. He pulled down the blankets, then covered me with a sheet after I stretched out. "I hope you don't mind if I sit here awhile."

"To watch me sleep?"

He nodded. "To reassure myself that you are really here and safe."

I didn't think I could sleep with him in the chair

next to my bed, but I did. When I woke, the sun sat low on the horizon. I stretched and tossed aside the sheet, surprised that Brock no longer sat in the chair.

I made my way through a dim house to the dining room where the others sat enjoying a meal of steak and baked potato. Ruthie had my plate in my hands before I sat down. "Thank you. I'm starving." I took my seat next to Brock. "Why are we sitting in the dark?"

"Morgan thought it would be harder for them to see our silhouettes and do a head count."

Smart thinking. "Shall I crawl on the floor?" I grinned around a mouthful of filet. "Shutterbug could use some company."

Morgan laughed. "No, but I do think it's a good idea that all three of you women not be in the same room at the same time. Lori has chosen to stay out of sight until bedtime."

"I'll take the night shift since I slept the day away." I stuck another bite of tender steak into my mouth.

"That leaves me with the day," Ruthie said. "Perfect."

"Where is Lori staying out of sight?"

"The guest room closet. We put a cot and a television in there. When the closet door is closed, no light gets through."

"The best place." Once a safe room, the code to lock the door lost to us before Ruthie purchased the home, the door blended with the wall paneling and became invisible. "I'm glad you haven't gotten around to fixing the lock."

"Someday." She smiled.

Next, I asked the question I knew had to be on everyone's mind. "How do we prove Warren's guilt and have him locked up if we're stuck in the house?"

"Banks is working on it," Morgan said. "He's also trying to get a shift as guard in order for me to sneak out for a while. I'll go for a jog again in the morning but can't be gone as long as I was today. Warren wanted to know how far I ran. I lied and said I stopped for a coffee and lost track of time. I'm pretty sure he'll have me watched a little closer now."

"I could go for a jog," Brock said. "I'm going stir-crazy sitting in the house. My agent is frothing at the mouth because filming has grounded to a halt over all this." He glanced at me. "But Louie is outraged. Said he doesn't understand why you can't do your job and be watched at the same time."

"But Warren said no." I slouched in my chair.

He sighed. "Warren told him you're a fugitive of the law and would be locked up again two seconds after they find you." He motioned to a paper on the table. "Your friend Susan is having a grand old time making up stories for the *Tribune*."

I glanced down to see the photo of Brock and me on the beach. I read, "From starlet to fugitive, what will Kelly Canyon do next?" I threw the paper down. "Good grief, the woman is a pain in my rear."

"No such thing as bad publicity, dear." Ruthie stood and gathered up the empty dishes. "If you make it through this latest adventure alive, you'll be the most sought-after actress in Hollywood.”

“Making it through *alive*, being the operative word here.” Maybe I should have bought a gun.

Chapter Twenty-three

I sat in the dark closet long after the others had gone to sleep and squirmed on the cot. If hiding was to become a habit, Ruthie would need to install a bathroom.

After my homeless adventure, I'd drunk a lot of water to make up for lost time. The house was dark. I stayed low.

I pushed open the closet door, ordered Shutterbug to stay, and peered into the guest bedroom. Nobody lurked around in there. From the room across the hall, Morgan's snores assured me everything was just fine.

I darted to the next door and quietly locked the door. Sweet relief. After washing my face and hands, I opened the door to repeat my stealthy return to the safe room.

A man in black, including the ski mask on his

face, blocked the door and held a finger to his lips. The very same man we'd encountered in the theater, not once but twice.

My heart dropped to my toes. A simple call of nature would be my demise. "Can I get my shoes?" I whispered.

He shook his head, waving the gun toward the back of the house. When I didn't move, he prodded me with the barrel.

Great. I considered knocking over a lamp on our way to the yard but decided against the small act of rebellion to protect my friends and family from being in the same boiling pot I was.

"Stop right there!" Lori blocked the back door.

Mr. Ski Mask held his gun to my head. "Shut up, drop the gun, and come with us, or I kill her right here for her grandmother to find."

Lori dropped the gun and backed out of the door. I was shoved through after her.

"Make it quick before someone wakes up." He herded us around the house to the gate and into a waiting dark blue van.

"Where's my dog?"

"Locked in that stupid room you came out of. Don't worry. I don't hurt animals." He bound Lori's hands with a zip tie behind her back, then mine.

As Morgan burst through the gate, our captor leaped into the driver's seat and careened down the driveway and onto the street. Shots sounded, and a bullet hit the side of the van. Our driver rounded a sharp corner, catapulting Lori and me across the back and into the opposite wall.

"Is my tracker still working?" I whispered,

struggling to a sitting position.

"I think so. Press your back against mine."

I did, and we used each other as leverage to sit upright. "Then they'll find us."

"Unless we're dead before they can reach us."

Good point. We had to stay alive. For the second time in less than twenty-four hours, I was in danger of getting killed. Not a habit I enjoyed.

The man drove us to a warehouse about an hour away, if my timing was right. Hard to tell sitting in the back of a van with no watch or clock. After parking, he threw open the van doors. "Get out." He wrenched my arm and dragged me out before doing the same with Lori.

I fell to the cracked asphalt. "Take it easy, dude."

"Shut up. You're going to be dead anyway." He yanked us to our feet and shoved us toward the building.

If looks could kill, he'd be dead from the fire in Lori's eyes as she hit the pavement. Now with ramrod shoulders, she marched ahead of us.

The interior of the concrete building smelled of mildew. A single bulb hung from a wire in the ceiling. Steel doors led in other directions, but our captor pushed us toward seats in the middle of the first room.

He squatted in front of us. "This is where I leave you. My job is done. The man who hired me will be along shortly. Enjoy the time you have left." He patted my cheek, too hard to be friendly, then stood and left, pulling the chain on the light on his way out and casting us into pitch black.

"Now what?" I said.

"Ever watch a video on how to get out of zip ties?" Lori shifted next to me.

"No, never had the need to, but I heard you use your shoe strings. I'm barefoot."

"Ah. Let me do this and I'll free you." More shuffling, some grunting, then a shout of glee. "Hold still while I find something to cut you loose. Oh, my gosh, something furry just ran across my hand."

"A rat?" My blood chilled. I tried to wrestle to my feet, hard to do with hands behind my back, but I finally succeeded. What if it ran across my bare feet? Bit my toe?

"There is absolutely nothing in this room," Lori said.

"Then let's get out of here and find something outside. We have to go before whoever shows up."

Her hand gripped my arm. "I have no idea which way is out."

"Pick a door. Any door." We shuffled through the dark, stopping when I slammed into a wall.

"I found a handle." The door creaked on rusty hinges as she pushed it open. A bit of moonlight came through a window with boards nailed across most of it, illuminating a hallway.

Another door behind us squeaked open. Lori pulled me close as the light in the room where we'd been deposited came on.

"Lawrence!" Warren yelled. "Don't make this any harder."

"We got our confirmation he's dirty," I said. "That's a subject we can put to rest."

"Oh, goody." Lori opened another door, then closed it behind us. A couple of crates sat next to the wall, and she pushed them in front of the door. "Hopefully, that will hold him off for a while."

I rubbed the zip ties against the sharp corner of a metal desk. They broke free, and I groaned. My shoulders ached, and my hands tingled as the blood rushed back into them. "We need a plan."

"The only plan I have is to keep us alive."

"I like that plan." I moved to the boarded-up window and tugged on a board. It loosened. I tugged harder. It fell in my hands, and I stumbled back. The sound seemed magnified. I held my breath and glanced at the door.

Warren knocked. "Not trying to escape, are you? You know I cannot let that happen."

"We were partners!" Lori leaned against the crates holding the door.

"You weren't supposed to be here." He pushed against the door.

I tugged with earnest on the boards over the window. All we had to do was avoid getting killed until Morgan showed up, hopefully with Jason and both of them armed to the teeth.

"Who are you working for?"

"Me, myself, and I."

"Ha." Lori motioned for me to go faster. "You aren't smart enough to have engineered this type of deception. Johnson?"

"He'll be here soon. You can ask him yourself."

I pulled the last board free and tried to shimmy through the tiny window. All I did was scrape up my ribcage. "It's too small."

"Try harder. You're tiny." Lori tried pushing me through.

"It's no use." I slid out and put a hand to my bleeding side. "We're stuck here."

"Once Johnson arrives, those crates won't hold them both out." Lori slid down, keeping her back to the crates. "Might as well sit it out and wait for another opportunity."

I sat next to her. "If we don't make it out, I want you to know that I'm happy to have met you. I'm glad Dad shared his life with you in the end."

She gripped my hand. "Don't give up yet. Morgan will come."

"I hope he comes in time."

"Me too." She kept hold of my hand. "Are you bleeding?" She released my hand and wiped her palm on her pants.

"A little bit. Just a scrape. Not all of the glass was out of the window."

"Did you ever think that as an actress you'd be in this situation?"

I laughed. "I never thought I'd be an actress."

"Your father would be proud of you. You would have made a good cop."

"And be in danger from criminals every day?" I chuckled.

"What's so funny?" Warren shoved against the door again.

We ignored him and stayed where we were. Women were better at the waiting game than men. As long as no one pointed a gun at us through the window I'd unboarded, we were good for a while.

"What do you think will happen to the studio

once Johnson is arrested?" Lori asked.

"No idea. Someone will buy it, I'm sure." I couldn't help but wonder if it would halt filming of our series for a while. Ruthie would be devastated. It had taken her a long time to make her comeback in Hollywood.

Me? Well, it had been a while since I'd sent any celebrity pictures to the *Tribune*'s competitor. I could make money that way again. Funny how I'd been so reluctant to pursue acting and would now miss it if it went away.

"Did you always want to be a cop?"

Lori nodded. "For as long as I can remember. I think in kindergarten I wanted to be a princess, but that didn't happen." She smiled.

"Doesn't it seem strange that there's a man on the other side of the door who wants to kill us and we're carrying on a conversation like we're having coffee and a doughnut?"

"A little."

Warren shoved against the door again and muttered something derogatory about Johnson being late. "I'm supposed to have you dead when he arrives, Canyon."

"Sorry I can't oblige you." He was getting on my nerves. "Just sit down and relax. We aren't coming out."

"Hey, Warren, be a dear and let me borrow your phone?" Lori grinned.

"Shut up."

"And to think we used to get along so well." She shook her head. "Not really. I never could stand the guy."

"I'm going to shoot you first, Lawrence."

"Oh, good. I'd hate to have to wait."

He fired a couple of rounds into the steel door. Thank you, God, it wasn't made of wood. Instead of being dead, I had ringing ears.

Lori glanced at her watch. "Three a.m. We've been living this adventure for four hours. Your tracker is only good for a little while longer."

"They'll find us. They will." My heart rate increased. Perspiration broke out on my forehead and upper lip. Was I having an anxiety attack? A heart attack? I'd never had either, but I'd never been this close to death before. Close, but not like this.

The dreaded tears sprang to my eyes. Stop it, Canyon. You are Kevin Canyon's daughter. You are not a quitter. I got to my feet, my scraped side burning. I'd fight as long as I could. I paced the room, my gaze searching every nook and cranny.

"What are you looking for?" Lori's brow furrowed.

"A weapon."

"I've already looked."

"I'm still going to search. We aren't going to be alone much longer." I moved aside boxes. Shoved aside loose sheets of paper, then found a nail. A long one used for construction. Not much, but it was better than nothing. I held it up and grinned.

"Good job." Lori crawled around searching for one for herself. "Got one. Hide it in your clothes."

I dropped it in my cleavage, the metal cool against my skin. The smell of rust rose and tickled my nostrils. It felt like safety.

"There you are."

I whirled and stared into a gun in the hand of Johnson, which pointed right at my head.

Chapter Twenty-Four

I dove as he pulled the trigger, knocking a stack of boxes down on top of me. Not much cover, but better than nothing. I scrambled behind the metal desk, praying Lori found a place to hide.

"I really hate to lose such an up-and-coming actress," Johnson said, "but your nosiness has risen to the point where you need to be eliminated. Nothing personal, Miss Canyon."

"Sorry to say, Mr. Johnson, but I take offense." I curled into as small a ball as possible. That made me less of a target, right? I thought I'd read that somewhere.

A quick peek over the top of the desk showed he'd left the room. A few minutes later, the door opened, inch-by-inch as the two men pushed against the obstacles. I pulled the nail from my bra. It wouldn't be much protection against a bullet, but if I could get close enough, I didn't think I'd have any problem jabbing it into one of them.

Lori crawled to my side. "Do not let them separate us."

"I don't plan on it. You take Warren, I'll take Johnson."

"My pleasure. I'd like nothing more than to stick this nail right into his lying eye."

"All right, ladies," Warren said, stepping around the desk. "Let's go."

"Go where?" I asked, offering him a shaky smile.

"Back to the room you were supposed to stay in. Much easier to clean up after ourselves in a big vacant room with a drain." He gave a feral grin.

Eww. I took a deep breath and rose to my feet. Lori and I would have to act fast.

I walked as slowly as I could back to the main room, Warren cursing under his breath the whole way. Johnson waited for us there and pointed to a large sheet of plastic.

"Stand there, please, and turn your backs to me," he said, motioning with his gun.

I glanced at Lori, then back at him. "You really expect us to make this easy for you?"

"I think you should look us in the eyes when you kill us," Lori said.

"Nobody is dying here today." Jason stepped through the door, a gun aimed at Warren.

"Unless it's you two men," Morgan said, joining him and aiming his gun at Johnson.

Warren grabbed Lori and positioned himself in front of her. Johnson did the same with me.

"Now!" Lori ducked and whirled, stabbing

Warren in the cheek.

Johnson was a bit faster, but I got the nail into his gun hand. I didn't need an invitation to run. I dashed from the room as the men started shooting.

Lori grabbed my hand and pulled me down the hall toward an outside door. "Stay out there." She led me to a squad car, opened the door, punched numbers into a keypad on the glove compartment, and then pulled out a gun. "I'll be back. Lock the doors."

I opened my mouth to protest, but the continuing firestorm in the building decided for me. This time I would let the authorities handle things.

A few minutes later, Morgan, pressing a hand to his shoulder, Jason holding on to his side, and Lori exited the building. I flung open the car door. "What happened?"

"It's over," Lori said. "Warren and Johnson are dead."

I sagged against the car. "We still don't know who Warren worked for, or even if there is someone else."

She rested a hand on my shoulder. "I'm certain there is a mastermind, but I don't think it was Warren."

Sirens wailed in the distance.

I turned as four police cars stopped next to us. The chief-of-police, Warren Foster, marched up to Banks, shooting a glare at Lori. "What happened here, Officer?"

Banks explained how they had rushed into save Lori and me. "We've suspected Warren took money for turning a blind eye to Johnson's dealings.

Officer Lawrence and Miss Canyon were a big help in taking down these criminals."

Foster glanced our way again. "Fine. Lawrence, you're back on duty. Miss Canyon, give your statement and go home. And, Lawrence, call an ambulance for Banks and this other man."

She grinned and tossed me a wink. "Yes, sir."

Morgan handed her his cell phone. "Glad to see you're reinstated."

"Me, too." She punched in the numbers required to call an ambulance. "One is already on the way," she said, hanging up. "Someone else reported the shooting."

I scanned the surrounding area. Jerard flashed a grin before disappearing into the shadow of a building opposite us. The young man might have tried to kill me at the beach house and blow up the Thunderbird, but it paid to have him on my side.

The ambulance arrived, and paramedics tended to Jason's and Morgan's gunshots and the scrape on my side which turned out to be deeper than I'd thought and required a couple of stitches. I shook my head. The place looked like a war zone.

The medical examiner's team wheeled Johnson and Warren out of the building in body bags. While my career as an actress might be up in the air, I couldn't mourn the death of the studio owner. The world was less one ruthless, immoral man. Two actually. Good riddance.

I opened the front door of my home to silence.

"Hello?"

"Back here." Brock's voice came through the locked door of Ruthie's bedroom.

Shutterbug whined and scratched, setting up a frenzy. I unlocked the door. "Why is the lock turned around?"

Brock pulled me against him. "To keep us from following. I'm going to punch Morgan in the face when I see him."

"You'll have to wait until morning." My words were muffled against his chest. "He's in the hospital."

"No." Ruthie put a hand to her mouth.

"If I can get some coffee, I'll explain everything."

Brock held me at arm's length. "You're wounded." He scooped me into his arms and deposited me on the sofa. "Ruthie, coffee."

Shutterbug laid her head on my feet and raised sad dark eyes. I reached down and scratched behind her ears. "I'm glad you weren't with me this time, girl. They would have killed you without a second thought."

Several minutes later, Ruthie thrust a mug of coffee into my hands. "Talk. Where's my Morgan?"

"No need." Morgan stepped into the room, followed by Jason. Morgan hobbled toward Ruthie. "Did you say *my* Morgan?"

She smiled, tears streaming down her face. "I did." She gripped his arms. "Are you all right?"

"I'm just fine." He lowered his head and kissed her.

"You?" Jason's gaze fell to the gauze around

my waist.

"I'm good. You?"

"Just a graze. Any more coffee, Grandma?"

"Oh, don't call her that," I said. "She doesn't like it."

"Jason saved my Kelly. He can call me anything he wants." Ruthie patted his cheek. "There is plenty of coffee. Sit so you can fill us in on this horrible adventure."

I rolled my eyes. I'd been her granddaughter far longer than she'd known Jason. But I wasn't a handsome young man, and Ruthie did like good-looking men.

"Don't leave me out." A showered Lori joined us.

Once everyone had coffee in hand and cookies Ruthie had pulled from the cupboard, Lori started talking. "When we escaped the main room and locked ourselves in some kind of office, I started to think Kelly's tracker wasn't working."

"It kept bleeping out," Morgan said. "I think the concrete building and high-voltage wires in the area messed with the signal. We found you by process of elimination."

"In the cliché'd eleventh hour." I raised my mug in a toast. "Thank you very much."

Ruthie snuggled up to Morgan's uninjured side. "I guess with Johnson dead, we have some time off. Let's take a vacation. Anyone up for Hawaii?"

Every hand raised.

"I need a couple of days first," I said. "There's something I need to do."

Chapter Twenty-five

I found Sarah in her culvert. When she spotted me, she jumped to her feet and wrapped me in a hug. "You made it through."

"You played a huge part in that." I returned the hug, then stepped back. "You ready to leave all this behind?"

Her brow furrowed. "There's one thing I want to keep." She rummaged in one of her crates and pulled out a snow globe. Amidst the glitter inside was an angel. "I found this little thing in the garbage years ago and held onto the hope it portrayed. We take everything else to the homeless community."

"Perfect. I brought help." I stepped aside as Brock ducked into the culvert.

"Oh my." Sarah's eyes widened as he took her hands in his. "You're Brock Handsome."

He laughed. "It's Hanson. I cannot thank you

enough for taking care of my lady when I couldn't."

"My pleasure," she said, her voice barely above a whisper. "You're going to give those in the community a heart attack."

Brock grinned and hefted one of the crates in his arms. "Shall we? I thought you might like a ride in a Jaguar."

She waved her hand. "Been there, done that."

"Good thing I hired a limo then." He winked and left us to follow.

I lifted the other crate, wincing as it pulled on my stitches, and carried it to the waiting black stretch limo. Won't the eyes of those at the community bug out when we pull up in this?

We stopped just outside of where the tents and cardboard boxes started. Sarah took a few things out of one of the crates. "I'd like to give some of my things to a few choice people. Some of these good folks helped me like I helped you." She strode away.

I leaned back against Brock. "I wish we could help them all."

He wrapped his arms around my waist. "I do, too. Maybe we could build a shelter."

"That's a great idea. We could interview some of the people here and hire them as staff." The idea held great possibilities.

When Sarah finished doling out her few articles of clothing, Brock told the driver to take us to the spa.

"Oh, I couldn't." Sarah protested, but the twinkle in her eyes belied her words.

Two hours later, I barely recognized the woman

standing in front of me. Her lightly peppered hair styled and highlighted. Her toes and nails polished and painted. A light application of makeup and she was ready to be introduced to Ruthie.

My grandmother didn't wait for introductions. She immediately grabbed the woman to her bosom and sobbed.

Sarah's frightened look over Ruthie's shoulder was priceless. When she finally pulled herself free, she smoothed her blouse. "It's nice to meet you, Ruthie Canyon. I'm a big fan."

"No, you're my dearest friend." Ruthie held the woman's hands. "You saved my girl. Come. I'll show you the kitchen."

Brock looped an arm around my shoulder. "I think more than one life was saved this week."

I raised my face for a kiss. "Agreed. Now kiss me before someone interrupts."

Don't miss the first two books:
A Hollywood Murder
Killer Pose, book 1
Killer Snapshot, book 2
Or
Kodak Kill Shot, book 4

Dear Reader,

I hope you are enjoying Kelly's and the group's escapades and mishaps as much as I love creating them. This book wrapped up the type of men William Johnson and Detective Warren were, but it didn't locate the one responsible for the murder of Kelly's father. I hope you stay tuned for book four, Kodak Kill Shot, which takes us further into Kelly's investigation.

With love,
Cynthia Hickey

Scan here for the next book, Kodak Kill Shot.

Chapter One

"I can't work if you're in my kitchen!" Sarah Doyles, recently homeless and now resident chef of Canyon Estates, whirled to face Ruthie, my grandmother and owner of said mansion, who'd given it the family name.

"It's my kitchen." Ruthie put her hands on her slim hips and glared. "You're nothing more than the hired help, and you're getting a bit too big for your apron."

I, Kelly Canyon, unwilling guest of the upcoming party tonight, sat at the table with a cup of coffee and prepared to watch the most entertaining thing I'd seen in a month. I smiled over the rim of my cup. These two had become best friends ever since Sarah saved my life. Sarah had been there when I had to pretend to be homeless to hide from an unscrupulous cop. But even the best of friends fight like tigers once in a while, and stress was running high today.

"You're the one with the big head." Sarah wiggled her fingers. "Give me the guest list and leave me alone."

Ruthie thrust over three pages of handwritten names in Sarah's direction. "I want fancy foods. We've a guest list of one hundred and fifty." She grinned, looking rather proud of herself. "Since Kelly's and my television show, *The Hart of Crime*, is nominated for an Emmy, everyone wants to be part of our clique."

Sarah rolled her eyes. "I'll dump the first platter of fancy food over your head if you don't hire me some help."

A laugh escaped me, turning both their glares on me. I pretended to cough.

"Bad acting, girl." Ruthie shook her head and stormed from the kitchen.

"How have you lived with her for so many years?" Sarah scanned the list of names in her hand.

"She isn't so bad—"

Sarah's face darkened. "She invited Robert? That cad—the man who ruined my life? I wouldn't serve him a platter of anything but slop fit for a pig." She tossed the list on the counter.

Ruthie wouldn't dare. I retrieved the papers. Yep. She'd invited the unscrupulous businessman, Robert Doyles, Sarah's ex-husband. Oh, grandma, what were you thinking?

After setting the papers on the counter, I went to look for some explanation. Ruthie sat on a sofa, knitting needles, her new fad, clicking at a remarkable pace. I doubted whether anything useable would result from her efforts, though. All I saw emerging was a tangled mess.

"What?" She didn't look up.

"Why did you invite Robert Doyles? You know

how Sarah feels about him."

Her hands stilled. "Because he provided some of the backing for our show. It's only right. She'll be in the kitchen and won't have to lay eyes on him."

"You still should have warned her."

The doorbell rang. As I headed to answer it, Ruthie said, "That would be the hired help I already got for that ungrateful woman in the kitchen."

I rolled my eyes and let in two kitchen helpers, who were informed by Ruthie that the wait staff would arrive one hour prior to the party's starting time, as would the bartender. "Are you having an open bar?" My eyes widened.

"Of course. This is Hollywood." She glanced up at me as if I'd lost my mind. "Our guests won't expect us to spare any expense. Don't worry. I'm footing the bill."

"I'll pay my share and be the official photographer, or did you hire one?"

"Of course, I hired one. You can't take photos in an evening gown. This is a formal party." Again, I got the look.

"You're always taking away my fun." Originally, my dream job was investigative journalist, and I'd worked for a tabloid until getting fired when I became a murder suspect. Then I found myself roped into acting, something I seemed to be good at, and took pictures of celebrity's pets as a side job. Now that I'd resigned myself to acting, I took photos as a hobby while trying to find my father's murderer. A full plate, but I'd never been happier. Especially since the first murder I'd gotten involved in had hooked Brock aka Handsome

Hanson, Hollywood's Golden Boy, as my boyfriend.

"You can act like a star for one night, Kelly." She set down her needles. "Look at it this way. No one is likely to kill one of us at our own party."

I hoped she hadn't just jinxed us.

At eight o'clock, I stood in an ice-blue, spaghetti-strapped gown that kissed the toes of my silver sandals and greeted guests as they entered our backyard. Lights floated in the pool along with giant magnolia blossoms. Glittering white lights hung from every surface holding a strand. The place had been transformed into a fairy land.

From the rapturous looks on the guests' faces, Ruthie had outdone herself. Hollywood would be talking about the party for weeks.

Paparazzi popped cameras over the fence in hopes of scoring a shot that would land on the first page of whatever tabloid they worked for. I smiled, remembering the frenzy of those days when selling a photo of a movie star paid my rent.

A soft whistle sounded behind me and I whirled around. Brock, resplendent in a black tux, strolled my way. "You look gorgeous." His arm snaked around my waist, and he pulled me in for a kiss.

"You aren't so bad yourself." I caressed his cheek.

"Sorry I'm late, but Morgan was worried about what to wear." He grinned.

I laughed, imagining the big man being nervous

about seeing Ruthie. The two were almost inseparable since the time they reconnected and she hired him as her bodyguard.

"If Ruthie does something this big over a nomination, I can't imagine what she'll throw if your show wins an Emmy."

"We'll find out soon enough." I seized his hand and led him to a pair of padded chaises in a secluded area of the yard. I shooed Shutterbug, my German shepherd, and Brutus, Brock's mastiff, from the furniture so we could sit. A yelp sounded from behind a pillow as I leaned back. I lurched up and glanced down at Sassy, Ruthie's Yorkie. "Sorry, girl."

The three dogs plopped on the ground, baleful eyes staring at us. "The chairs are for guests," I said. Sassy yelped her displeasure, bringing Ruthie running.

"What did you do to my baby?" She scooped up the dog.

"Moved her off the furniture."

"Come on, baby. Let's go find Morgan. He'll protect you from the evil Kelly." She glared at me and stormed away.

I sighed. "She's been like this all day. I think hosting this big of a party is too much for her."

"Maybe there's more on her mind than the party."

"Hmm." I accepted a glass of champagne from a waiter and leaned back. I'd received our guests, now they could fend for themselves. Schmoozing was the part of Hollywood I disliked the most, and I was no good at it.

"Come on." Brock held out his hand. "Let's walk. Let people see how beautiful you are, then we'll find a place away from it all." He winked. "Maybe I can get some kisses."

"If you're a good boy." I laughed and let him lead me away from my comfortable corner. The dogs immediately took our spots. At least we'd have somewhere to sit when we were ready.

Loud voices from outside the kitchen door drew us. Ruthie wouldn't tolerate a fight. I'd have to curb tempers before things got out of hand.

We turned the corner. Sarah was poking the chest of a distinguished man in a tux. "I turned out alright despite your cheating ways and unwillingness to spend one cent of your precious money to help me. I regret the day I ever laid eyes on you."

Ah, the infamous ex-husband, cheater and all-around horrible person. I stepped between them. "What's going on?"

"He came to the kitchen wanting to talk." Sarah crossed her arms. A whiff of alcohol wafted from her breath. "Since I don't want the world knowing my business, we took it outside. Now, tell him to go."

"Sarah…" Robert held out his hands. "I came to apologize."

"Really?" Her eyebrows rose. "Why? Because I now work for one of Hollywood's elite? Aiming to home in on my success?"

He laughed. "You're a cook."

"A mighty fine cook." She two-hand shoved him. "I don't ever want to see you again. I wouldn't shed a tear if you dropped dead. Nor do I care if that floozy you married after you dumped me shares a cent of your money. I don't want anything." Head high, she marched into the house.

He pivoted toward us. "I really did come to apologize."

"Some things can't be resolved. Come on, Mr. Doyles. There's a party happening." I glanced at Sarah, who was watching from the kitchen window as we led him away from the house and toward the pool. A flicker of alarm passed through me about the scent of alcohol on Sarah's breath. Ruthie loved her wine, but she wouldn't tolerate a drunk.

As we neared the area where the majority of the guests mingled, Robert halted. "I need time alone."

"May I ask why it's so important that Sarah speak with you? It didn't seem important enough when she lived on the streets and could have actually used help from you." I narrowed my eyes.

He sighed. "I have some money that belongs to her from a wealthy uncle of hers that died recently. If my wife finds out about it, she'd badger me to give it to her. The woman is draining me dry."

"So, you were hoping Sarah would share this inheritance with you?"

"Of course. If a woman is entitled to half of what a man has after ten years of marriage, why can't it swing the other way? Would you tell her for me? She might listen to you."

I nodded as he strolled toward the rose bushes at the opposite end of the pool. In a tux, broke and needing money. Such an over-told story.

"I knew it." Sarah hissed from behind a tree. "I

knew he'd spill his guts to you, and it had to do with money. He'll not get a penny of what's mine."

"That isn't like you, Sarah." I felt as if I didn't know this bitter woman. The Sarah I knew was kind, loving, and nurturing. "You've been drinking."

"I took a little to get up the nerve to face him." Tears welled in her eyes. "You're right. It isn't me. That man brings out the worst in me." She rushed away.

"Life is never boring around the Canyons," Brock said.

"No, it isn't. Can we go find a place to sit?"

"I'd like nothing better."

We returned to our little alcove. This time, rather than move the dogs, we snuggled onto the lounge chairs with them. Nothing calmed rattled nerves like the unconditional love of an animal.

I must have fallen asleep, completely shirking my hostess duties, because when I opened my eyes, Ruthie stared down at me. "It's three a.m. You completely missed the party. Everyone noticed. There must be a hundred cell-phone photos of you sleeping."

I stretched. "I'm sorry. I didn't realize how tired I was." I glanced to where Brock slept and smiled. He looked so boyish when he was asleep. "I only intended to hide away for a little while. How was the party?"

"A complete success." She grinned. "Everyone had a good time. We even had some skinny-dipping. I was about to change and take a dip myself to soothe away the pain in my feet from these shoes."

"That sounds like a great idea."

Fifteen minutes later, wearing my favorite navy-blue suit, I raced for the pool's edge and skidded to a halt. Robert Doyles floated facedown among the magnolia blossoms.

www.cynthiahickey.com

Cynthia Hickey is a multi-published and best-selling author of cozy mysteries and romantic suspense. She has taught writing at many conferences and small writing retreats. She and her husband run the publishing press, Winged Publications. They live in Arizona and Arkansas, becoming snowbirds with three dogs. They have ten grandchildren who keep them busy and tell everyone they know that "Nana is a writer."

www.ingramcontent.com/pod-product-compliance
Lightning Source LLC
Chambersburg PA
CBHW061036120726
47910CB00006B/2270